Yearn for Blood

Blood Origin Series

Book 1

Tiffany Heiser

Willow Moon Publishing

Copyright © 2018 by Tiffany Heiser Published by Willow Moon Publishing 108 Saint Thomas Road Lancaster, PA 17601 willow-moon-publishing.com

Cataloging Data Heiser, Tiffany (1984-) Yearn for Blood/Tiffany Heiser–

2ndU.S. Edition

Summary: Rena's world takes a turn into the supernatural when she finds out Cryder is not human and is destined to be with her. His destiny is irrevocably linked to Rena's. She's forced to jump into this supernatural world without the time to consider the possibilities of this new world with vampires, because it looks like Cryder has brought more than his mysterious demeanor, but a rogue vampire hell-bent on taking her blood for his own. There's nowhere to run, so Rena must learn to fight back and become the true person she was meant to be.

149 pages; 216 x 140 mm Hardcover ISBN-13: 978-1-9482563-08
1.YoungAdult/Fiction/Romance/Paranormal.2.YoungAdult/Fiction/Roman ce/Vampires 3. Young Adult/Fiction/Romance/General Yearn for Blood. Heiser, Tiffany Printed in the United States on acid free paper Typeset: Sabon NextLT Edited by Kat Helgeson Design by Jodi Stapler

This is dedicated to my Grandma Meme, for reading and being a big fan from the beginning; For giving the best compliment... not being a reader yourself, and yet staying up late to finish my book. And for being in love with my writing, I thank you.

ACKNOWLEDGEMENTS

I'd like to thank my family and friends, those that took time to read what I wrote and to continue to push me. For those that have been walking with me through the process and stayed on the phone to listen to ideas, or long-winded ramblings; I adore and appreciate each one of you and give my many thanks for the support and love.

CONTENTS

Prologue

MY MIND WAS THE FIRST THING TO WAKE AND never in my life had I been so afraid. I was awake, or at least I thought I was, so why did every part of me feel so strange, so disconnected? I tried to move but all my limbs were unresponsive. My toes wouldn't wiggle; my legs wouldn't shift; my head wouldn't turn. I was lost in my mind—trapped within my own body.

I stupidly cried out for help, as if there were someone in my consciousness who could hear and save me. As if I wasn't completely alone. Over and over again, I screamed, but when no one answered, I forced myself to calm down and push the fear that threatened to drown me to a tolerable level. Think. What was happening to me? I was awake. I had to be awake because I was thinking coherent thoughts and then it finally dawned upon me: sleep paralysis.

I remembered looking into the subject after Cecile had mentioned it one day, and it was the most logical answer. I was awake and aware, but I couldn't physically move, and the only way to remedy sleep paralysis was, much to my dismay, to wait. It felt like an eternity as I waited anxiously with my thoughts, but sure enough, my senses slowly began to return. It started off with a dull and insistent ringing in my ears—annoying under usual circumstances, but right now a relief. Then, I could feel. My fingers twitched against a soft but unfamiliar material underneath my hands, followed by my forehead. I immediately tried to open my eyes. They felt like heavy curtains; however, my persistence paid off, and the tiny muscles around my eyes finally engaged in lifting them. I could've laughed, I was so happy for this freedom.

But then my awareness shifted to a deep ache lurking somewhere inside my body, and it hit me: something was wrong.

My eyes finally fluttered open, and darkness greeted me like an old friend. For a moment, I stared dumbly at it, not understanding why I had woken up to darkness again panic I'd managed to push down earlier rose within me like the tide. What's wrong with me? Where am I? With my sight taken away, my other senses were heightened, and they focused on whatever stimulant they could get, which so happened to be the ringing in my ears. It grew louder and louder like a busy hive of bees and only when I finally started to think that it was annoying, did I notice another sound.

A faint beeping disturbed the monotonous ringing, and my attention latched on to it. The sound was steady and louder in one ear than the other, so I instinctively turned towards it, with some difficulty. My neck felt stiff as I rolled my head heavily towards the noise, and, much to my relief, saw the blurry outline of a small green light. I wasn't blind. I squinted at the tiny orb, trying to figure out what it was, but my eyes were slow to adjust, and I eventually settled on just listening to the beeping. It was steady and reassuring, a reminder that I was alive.

But then I realized it was my heartbeat I was listening to, and like a freight train, reality hit me.

My breath hitched as a deep and painful ache flared through my body like wildfire, and I clutched at the soft sheets underneath my hands. I wanted to scream, but my mouth was so dry that my tongue stuck to the roof. I ground my teeth tightly together and fought to control my sudden pain. Once I managed to, I sucked in a breath and registered the scent of latex and harsh cleaning chemicals, which overwhelmed me and made my stomach lurch. I forced myself to keep breathing the nauseating scent in, not wanting to pass out and become trapped in my mind again.

When my pain was more manageable, I tried to sit up. But a sharp twinge of pain shot up my arm, and I immediately plopped back down onto my back. Lifting my arm, I blindly groped the crook of my elbow, where what felt like wires were taped to my skin. I tugged at them experientially and winced when they refused to budge, then slid my hand farther down my arm. I fumbled with my other hand and felt a clip on my finger that had to be the heart monitor.

Hospital. I'm in a hospital. But why? How did I end up here? I couldn't remember anything.

"M-mom?" I croaked dryly, my voice so low and scratchy that I wasn't sure anyone would be able to hear me, even if there was someone nearby. No answer.

"Mom?" I tried again. When there was still only silence, panic seized me again. I can't breathe. I tugged at the flimsy gown I wore; it was choking me. My mind barely registered the way the heart monitor's beeping increased, but what my mind did register in vivid detail was the door opening and the room suddenly flooding with light. It burned my eyes, and I cried out in a mixture of fear and pain, raising my arms to block it.

"Shhh, shhh..." A soft voice cooed urgently at me, and I felt hands rubbing my arm and shoulder. "It's going to be alright, sweetie. You're safe. You're at the hospital, and we're going to take care of you."

I peeked through my arms at the woman suddenly at my side, and my eyes were instantly drawn to the pink polka dot scrubs she wore – a nurse. I allowed her to settle me back into bed and watched as she adjusted a knob on one of the machines connected to my arm. When she started to move away, I quickly reached out and snatched her by the hand. "Where's my mom? Please, I want my mom."

Her hand tightened around mine, and she took a moment to tuck a lock of curly dark hair behind her ear before her warm brown eyes looked into mine. "It's going to be alright, sweetie." she repeated. "The doctor will be in soon, and he'll be able to explain everything to you."

I shook my head, not satisfied by her answer, "Please! Tell me now! Can you tell me anything? I don't even know why I'm here!"

The nurse pursed her lips and looked at me hesitantly. It was obvious that she was conflicted and wanted to help me. "You were in an accident… A few scrapes and bruises, you were very lucky. You've been here since then, asleep. We put in a saline drip to make sure you didn't dehydrate. Everything else will have to come from the doctor." She paused, looking down at me. "I'm so sorry, sweetie."

I stared at her, trying to remember the accident, but I came up blank. I looked away from the nurse and gnawed anxiously at my bottom lip. "My parents…?" I unintentionally whimpered as my lips quivered. Hot tears slipped from my eyes and slid down my cheeks. "Can you tell me anything about my parents? A-are they okay?"

The nurse's hold on my hand tightened, and she refused to meet my eyes. Her lips parted for a moment, and then she closed them again. When the words finally escaped her, the low, solemn tone she spoke in answered my question even though her words didn't. "Let me go get the doctor now. I'm not allowed to say anything else. I'm so sorry." With that, she walked out of the room.

The door closed behind her with a quiet click, leaving me alone with thoughts of denial running wild in my mind. She's wrong…nothing happened…everything's fine… But a dam inside me had broken, and tears flowed from my eyes like a rushing river. When the doctor walked in, I tried to compose myself and be brave. I rubbed my eyes vigorously, trying to wipe the tears away, but they wouldn't stop.

The concerned looks on the nurse's and doctor's face reaffirmed what I had concluded, and I tried to listen to what he had to say, but the world around me had become a disembodied blur. I had lost everything. I had lost everyone. How I had survived the accident was beyond me, and I should have been thankful that I was still alive, but I wasn't.

I was only grateful that I wasn't awake to see my parents die.

Chapter One

MAKING MY WAY DOWNSTAIRS AFTER GROGGILY finishing up my morning routine, the sweet aroma of French toast filled my nose and called me into the kitchen. I was greeted by the familiar sight of a short woman with thinning blonde hair by the stove. My stomach must have growled louder than I thought it did as I watched Mrs. Danvers flip an egg-y slice, because she turned and smiled at me with one of the only two bright smiles I could tolerate so early in the morning.

"Morning, sour puss!" she teased me with the morning nickname she had given me since I was little. "French toast?"

I nodded my head as I pulled a seat out from the counter. Besides Cecile, Mrs. Danvers knew that I was a borderline insufferable grouch in the mornings without food or caffeine in my system, and she knew just how to take care of me. Minutes after I had settled in, she set a plate of freshly made French toast sprinkled with powdered sugar in front of me and poured me a cup of coffee. I would have kissed Cecile's mom for being the most valuable player in the world, but food and coffee took precedence in my life. I mumbled a quick "Thank you" to Mrs. Danvers before I seized the syrup dispenser and resisted the urge to cradle it in my hands when I discovered that it was warm. Even after so many years, I was still amazed by the level of effort she put into her cooking, and I greedily poured the syrup over my plate before exchanging it for the vanilla creamer.

I was four bites into my breakfast when I heard a flurry of steps down the stairs and turned just in time to see Cecile rush into the kitchen. On a scale of one to ten, Cecile was a solid nine, and I was a four on a good day. Her blonde hair was always straightened to perfection, and her make-up was so flawless that I wasn't entirely convinced that she didn't have a professional locked away in her room. Compared to me, Cecile always looked like she had just stepped out of a fashion magazine. Whereas I had thrown on an old t-shirt and jeans, with just enough eyeliner to give off the appearance of having my life together. I couldn't help feeling a little self-conscious. There had always been a noticeable difference between us, and puberty had been kinder to her than me, but our friendship had always been strong, even after boys started entering the picture.

"We're having French toast," I informed her after swallowing a mouthful and pulled out the seat next to me.

Cecile shot me a smile, the only other bright smile I could tolerate in the morning, as she strolled over to Mrs. Danvers and planted a kiss on her mom's chubby cheek. "I know! I could smell it from upstairs. Mom was a tease all morning, so I had to rush to make sure I had time to get some."

I quirked an eyebrow at her and gestured to all of her with my fork, "That's rushing?"

She laughed as she poured herself a cup of coffee and plopped down next to me. "You know me. I could have taken more time finishing up—Mom, not too much!"

I smiled at Cecile's outburst, feeling more human now that

there was food and caffeine in me, and watched as she tried to convince her mom to not put too many slices of French toast on her plate. This was every day in the Danvers' Household, and I loved it. Our parents were friends before Cecile and I were even born, so I supposed that it was only natural that we would grow up together to be like sisters. I couldn't imagine a life without Cecile, and I owed her and her parents everything. After my parents died two years ago, they were the only things that kept me going. They took me under their wings and opened their home and hearts to me; they gave me space when I needed it and affection when I craved it. I was family to them, and they were family to me.

I was the first to finish my food, and I took my dishes to the sink to wash them despite Mrs. Danvers' protests. Compared to everything else that the Danvers had done for me, washing the dishes was a little thing but one of the few ways I could show how much I appreciated them. When I finished, I grabbed my bag and waited by the door for Cecile to say goodbye to her mom. I tried not to feel too envious as I watched the two from the corner of my eye exchange hugs and kisses, but I would have been lying if I said I wasn't just a bit jealous.

"Ready to go?' I asked Cecile with a small smile as I grabbed my bag and opened the front door. I waited for a moment to let her walk out first and just as I was about to wave good-bye to Mrs. Danvers, she called out to me. The moment I turned to look at her, I was engulfed in a warm embrace scented with cinnamon. A smile crossed my face. For someone so short, Mrs. Danvers was a fast lady. I returned the hug and smiled even wider when she placed a kiss atop my head.

"Have a good day, sweetheart. I'll see you after school," she whispered and rocked me side to side slightly.

"Thanks, Mrs. D. Have a good day," I whispered in reply,

relishing the human contact, and finally turned to walk out of the house after Cecile, who was lowering the top of her red convertible.

"Don't you think it's a bit chilly to be driving with the top down?" I asked, even though I didn't really care either way, and tossed my bag in the back to join hers.

"It's not that cold, plus it's been so long since the sun's been out! We need to take advantage of it while we can!" Cecile cheerily replied as she flipped through her phone to find a song to drive to.

I laughed in agreement and slipped into the passenger seat beside her before grabbing the pair of sunglasses I kept stashed away in the glove compartment.

We sped through the neighborhood on our way to school to the tune of an obnoxiously upbeat pop song, and I couldn't help but grin at the way Cecile bobbed to it when she thought no one was looking. I let my eyes drift away, giving her some privacy, and watched as the world around us passed in a blur before letting my head drop back against the chair to look at the sky. It had been a long time since the rain had stopped and despite the cold, it was a beautiful day. The air was clean and crisp like it always is after a long rain and the sky was so clear and blue that I wanted to fall up into it.

Until suddenly I really was falling.

I barely heard Cecile's high-pitched gasp before the weightlessness gripped me and my body lurched forward. A frightened squeak escaped my throat, but it was cut off when the seat belt locked firmly in place around my chest to keep me from flying out of my seat, and my hand shot out to slam against the dash. The screeching of tires and blaring of horns assaulted my ears, louder than my alarm clock could ever, and I clutched at the seatbelt in a death grip. I gasped for air, my heart pounding like mad inside my chest, a cold sweat forming on the back of my neck.

"—ena? Rena?"

Cecile's disembodied voice slowly became clearer in my ears, and I finally looked up at her, shaken. "I'm… I'm alright." I gasped unconvincingly and finally looked around. "W-what happened?"

"That jerk cut us off!" Cecile shouted and waved her fist angrily at a tinted black Ford Mustang speeding away in front of us. She turned back towards me; her pretty face wrinkled with worry. "I'm so sorry! Are you sure you're alright?"

I forced a half-hearted smile and nodded, but in truth I wasn't entirely sure. My skin felt clammy, and my limbs tingly as blood returned to them, but my pounding heartbeat wouldn't slow. The anxiety, the panic, the bad memories of the last car accident I was in were surfacing again, clawing their way back to the surface. You're okay…everything's fine…you're alive and so is Cecile.

With slow, deep breathing, I managed to calm down as we trailed after the car that Cecile had almost crashed into. But for some reason, I couldn't quite shake off another nagging feeling, underneath the anxiety I'd been trying to escape for so long.

The feeling that I was being watched.

Chapter Two

WE MADE IT TO SCHOOL WITHOUT ANY MORE close calls, but my heart still pounded in my chest. Uneasy, restless. Cecile pulled into the closest parking spot to school, and the moment she put her car into park I was on the move. The seat belt flew from around my body and clanked loudly against the door of the convertible before I shoved it open and almost slammed it against the neighboring car. I scrambled out, pausing only to snatch my bag from the backseat just as the top was beginning to climb back over, and took a few steps back.

"Rena?' Cecile's muffled voice called out to me before she popped out from the other side of the car. Her blue eyes peered worriedly at me as she watched me round the car to her side. "Are you sure you're alright?'

"Y-yeah," I lied, trying to keep my voice even and light, but I could tell from the way her brow pinched together she didn't believe me. The cons of being friends with someone for so long—she could read me like a book. She fell into step beside me and together we began walking towards our first period. "I'm okay," I meekly reassured her. "Really, I am. Just a little shaken, that's all."

It's just the adrenaline, I thought, even as my stomach roiled with nausea. The air around me grew more humid as the sun began to heat up the day, and the thickness of it felt suffocating. I looked toward the shaded sidewalk, only a few steps away, and urged myself forward faster, hoping I would feel better once out of the sun.

But the next thing I knew, the world around me swayed violently and my vision blurred.

My foot caught the curb of the sidewalk, and I stumbled forward with a startled gasp. Cecile cried out in surprise as my hands shot out in front of me, and I caught myself against a tree. The rough bark dug painfully into the palms of my hands and still I clutched at it, trying to anchor myself. My body swayed sickeningly side to side as if I were on the deck of a ship in the middle of a storm. I groaned as my stomach churned violently and threatened to spew my breakfast. My head throbbed and beads of sweat trickled down my forehead, forming a damp trail to my neck.

Slowly, I slid down to crouch at the base of the tree. I had no idea how long I knelt there, praying for what had to be a severe migraine to stop before I heard Cecile's far off voice.

"Rena!" She called my name out repeatedly, and I

snapped back to reality when I felt her shake my shoulders with more strength than someone her size should be able to muster. "What's wrong? Are you alright? Should I get a teacher?" She fired question after question at me, wanting to help but not giving me a chance to even answer.

I blinked warily at her, my vision still swimming, and swallowed audibly. "N-no," my voice shook, "I think it's just the heat." I brushed away the strands of dark hair from my face and took her offered hand. Cecile hoisted me up and gripped my elbow tightly as I swayed dizzily for a moment. "I'll feel better in some air conditioning. The humidity must be getting to me."

She looked at me skeptically before firmly hooking our arms, forcing me to lean against her. "Alright…" She didn't believe me one bit. "But I'm going to tell Mrs. Dawson you're not feeling too hot."

I wanted to argue with Cecile and let her know that she didn't have to go that far, but she was her mother's daughter and in turn, a worrywart. She escorted me to class as the final bell rang and left me at my desk before she walked to Mrs. Dawson and began speaking in a hushed voice. I couldn't hear their exchange from my desk, but I could see that Mrs. Dawson was hooked on every word she said. Cecile had a way with people, and everyone seemed to like her. With just a few words and a carefully timed smile, she could get anyone to do just about anything for her. I averted my eyes sheepishly when Mrs. Dawson looked in my direction, hating that I was the topic of their discussion, and watched through the corner of my eye as she nodded to Cecile and motioned for her to take her seat.

"Alright, guys and gals!" Mrs. Dawson chimed with a bright smile after Cecile sat down, "welcome back from the weekend! I thought we could go ahead and start this week off slow, so I decided that we're going to start watching Beastly. This is a new take on Beauty and the Beast, but pay attention to the details! I'm not showing this for you to have nap time. There will be a test on this comparing it to the reading sometime soon," she finished ominously as she pulled down the projector and started the film.

The moment the lights in the room dimmed, my mind started to wander. I had seen the movie before, and I knew the story well enough that it didn't warrant my complete attention. I watched absently as the two protagonists met. Despite the film being a little cheesy and cliché, I couldn't help injecting myself into the scenario and fantasizing about it all. True love's kiss, a curse breaking, a happy ending... Boy oh boy did I want to be romanced by a handsome boy and fall in love.

But while it was nice to fantasize about it all, the idea of actually being in a relationship made me wary. Maybe it was that I'd been the observant third wheel for Cecile's string of boyfriends for so long, but any time a boy expressed interest in me, I found myself stand-offish, knowing how it would likely end. Signing up to be a victim of a broken heart? No, thank you. Still, I couldn't help wondering how nice it would be to get the kind of happily ever after I'd read about so many times

-ena?

I jumped slightly in surprise when I heard my name being whispered and glanced directly in Cecile's direction, but she was paying attention to her cell phone. Everyone else watched the movie.

You can hear me, can't you?

The whisper made my skin crawl and the hair on my arms stand at attention, and I surveyed the room closer than I did before. Most eyes were glued to the movie; others were closed while their owners napped shamelessly. I must be imagining things, I thought, shaking my head. I slowly returned my attention to the film—or tried to, at least, but that uneasy feeling was rising in my stomach again. A flicker out of the corner of my eye made me jump, but it was just the light pouring in from the small window in the door. Drawn to it, I turned my head to peer against the light and saw a figure just outside shadowed by the sun.

In a flash, the world started to sway violently again. My breath hitched in my throat as the ceiling went in one direction while the floor went in the other. Unable to maintain my balance, I tumbled gracelessly from my seat and onto the floor with a loud thunk. Pain radiated dully up my arms and legs from falling so hard. Fortunately, the room stopped moving.

Wincing, I looked up to see every single one of my classmates had turned in their seat to gawk at me.

Mrs. Dawson rushed to my side, her skirt swaying like a

whirlwind, and knelt down beside me. "Rena, what happened? Are you okay?"

My cheeks burned with embarrassment, and I kept my eyes down on the floor in an attempt to escape the curious stares and Cecile's particularly penetrating one. "N-no, ma'am," I mumbled, thankful when my hair slipped from behind my shoulder to hang around my face like a curtain. "I think I'm coming down with something. Can I—may I go to the nurse's office?"

"Yes, of course. I think that would probably be best. Let me write you a pass and have someone escort you." Mrs. Dawson replied and started to look around the room for someone to escort me.

"No!" I squeaked in protest. "I can make it there by myself. I don't want anyone to miss out on the movie when there's going to be a test on it. The nurse's office isn't even that far. I can make it there." I looked up at her with begging eyes, praying that she would let me go alone so I could recover from my embarrassment, and sighed in relief when she relented. As Mrs. Dawson walked back to her desk to write me a pass, I mashed my folder into my backpack and almost snatched the paper from her when she returned with it. I mumbled "Thank you" and rushed to flee the room, pausing only for a moment for a quick glance in Cecile's direction, knowing that she would find me the moment class was over.

I hurried across the school's quad and entered the nurse's office, where I was forced to endure being poked and prodded at for several minutes. After she determined that I was a little warm, she handed me an ice pack to snuggle with and ordered that I rest until next period.

She dimmed the lights in the room and left me to lie there in the dark. I sighed, letting my eyes close. The almost-accident that morning had sure done a number on me, but I was convinced getting some rest would help me get back to normal. I was just still shaken; I needed to calm down. Relax. Then I'd stop imagining whispers that weren't real.

My mind soon began to drift. I was somewhere between consciousness and sleep when a figure stepped into my narrowing vision. I frowned tiredly. With the room being so dark, it was difficult for me to make out any exact details of who it was. Just when I was about to give up, the figure moved close enough for me to make out that it was a boy.

My eyes were instantly drawn to his piercingly bright blue eyes; a shiver ran down my spine from that strong, captivating gaze. I shifted my own eyes away, uncomfortable with meeting his gaze so familiarly, and trailed along his handsomely chiseled jaw to the dark locks of hair that framed his face. His full lips turned upwards into a grin when he caught me taking him in, and my heart thumped noticeably in my chest.

"Hello?" I whispered hesitantly, my voice practically shattering the silence in the room. He didn't answer my greeting, and I frowned, mildly disappointed. "Who are you?"

A loud knock on the door startled me, and I shot up from bed with a gasp. I looked towards the door just as it opened to let Cecile in before turning back to where the boy had been standing and frowned when I discovered I was the only one in the room. I must have been sleeping and dreamed it all...

"I brought you a snack," Cecile announced softly and held out a bag of cookies and a Gatorade out to me.

"Thanks, you didn't have to." I smiled appreciatively and took them from her before holding them in my lap. I wasn't feeling very hungry.

She waved her hand dismissively and plopped down on the bed next to me. "I was really worried. Maybe I should call mom and ask her to take you home?"

I shook my head. "No, I think I managed to sleep it off. I feel better, honest." She twisted her mouth again, disbelieving, and I leaned forward to wrap my arms tightly around her in a bear hug to show that I wasn't feeling as weak as I was earlier. "See?" I grinned when she laughed and returned my hug. "I'm not sure what was going on earlier, I just felt really off since we almost got in an accident. The nurse thinks I'm probably dehydrated." When we released each other from the hug, I made a point to take a drink from the Gatorade she had brought me to show that I was making an effort to get better.

"That makes sense. I always feel like I'm dying during practice when I don't drink enough water. No more soda and coffee for you! Just water!" Cecile tried to give me a stern look, one that resembled her mom's, but it lasted less than a second when she burst into a fit of giggles.

I laughed at her valiant attempt to channel Mrs. Danvers. "Yes, ma'am. I will do that." I mock saluted her before I swung my legs over the edge of the bed. "What time are we leaving today?" I asked as I picked up my bag to get ready to go to class again.

Cecile scrunched her nose and pursed her lips as if she just remembered something. "I forgot that I have cheer practice tonight, so I won't be able to drive you home right after school. I even need to run home during lunch to pick up my gear. I can ask Mom to pick you up when school is over, or maybe you can drive home and then pick me up?"
I blanched at the idea of driving, especially after the close call on the way to school, and I shook my head. "I don't think so. I don't even have my driver's license yet, remember?" It took a long time after the accident with my parents for me to gather the courage to get into a car again, and it was taking even longer for me to get behind the wheel itself. I knew it was a nuisance for Cecile and her family to drive me everywhere, but every time I got behind the wheel to drive, I just froze. I couldn't even turn the engine on. The fear of getting in another accident was paralyzing — worse, that I might be the cause of an accident where someone would die.

"You know what?' I said. "I'll just walk to Book City, and you can pick me up from there if it's not too much of a hassle."

Cecile nodded her head as the warning bell rang and we walked out of the nurse's office. "Yeah, that's not a problem. I won't see you until then since I have to drive back home during lunch, but I'll text you if anything changes."

"Alright, you know where to find me." I smiled as I gave her a quick hug.

"With a dreamy, far-off look, and her nose stuck in a book!'" Cecile sang out to me as she turned to rush off to class, and I couldn't help but laugh at how she quoted another version of Beauty and the Beast.

Chapter Three

BOOK CITY WAS A FIVE-MINUTE WALK FROM school, and by the time I got there I was feeling more like myself. The prospect of an afternoon at the bookstore, among musty old books, always had a rejuvenating effect on me. Plus, I was craving it all the more after so much talk of Beauty and the Beast — it was easy to understand the appeal books held for Belle, a girl bored by the everyday routine of her life. Sometimes I wished I'd be swept into a crazy adventure like she was.

The bookstore was charming, independently owned by a woman who knew the names of all her regulars. "Good afternoon, Rena!" she called as the bell announced my entrance.

"Afternoon, Ms. Kate." Sometimes I thought she was psychic. I couldn't even see where she was in the store, but she immediately knew it was me.

With a grunt, she emerged from behind a pile of boxes. "I just got off the phone with that sister of yours."

Oh. That explained it. "You know Cecile isn't my sister, Ms. Kate."

She waved her hand as if dismissing an unimportant detail. "She said you'd be spending the afternoon with me and I was to keep you out of trouble."

I snorted at that. "I've never been in trouble a day in my life."

"Don't I know it. You could do with a little trouble, if you ask me!"

I grinned. "I'll be in the back, okay?'

"Come find me if you want some coffee!"

I would have liked to sit and talk over a mug, but I remembered Cecile's admonition to stay away from coffee for the rest of the day. "Yes, ma'am," I said, knowing I wouldn't.

The back third of Book City was home to the Young Adult section, which was the main reason why it was my favorite bookstore in town. The big chains had one or two shelves of YA, but here it was an entire room, one a person could really immerse herself in and get lost. I liked to start in one corner and work my way all the way around, pulling out anything that caught my eye. It was important to set myself a limit or I might walk out of here with a dozen new books I couldn't afford. Two, I told myself firmly. No more than two today. My parents had left behind an inheritance for me, but no one had ever told me the amount. Cecile's mother gave me a weekly allowance from the account, and I had a bit saved up to spend, but I definitely didn't want to go broke today.

By the time I reached the back wall of the room,

though, I was already in a bind. I had three books tucked under one arm and a fourth in hand. There were just so many, was the problem—so many possible adventures to enter, so many characters to meet. How was I supposed to leave some of them behind? I put my nose to the pages and inhaled, breathing in the comforting smell of ink and glue, trying to determine which book had the best aroma.

"Um, are you okay?" said a voice from behind me.

My head jerked up, blood rushing to my cheeks. I'd been caught smelling books before; people always thought it was weird. God, I needed to stop doing that in public.

I turned to see a guy leaning nonchalantly against a rack of books, his arms folded across his beefy chest. He had the build of a linebacker—huge, all muscle padded in gut, like he was preparing to knock over anything that had the misfortune of being in his path. And yet, there was something appealing about him. Maybe it was the spark in his hazel eyes or the way his dark brown hair seemed to call out to be touched. Maybe it was the dimple that appeared in his cheek as he smirked at me. Maybe it was just that air of easy confidence. I was a sucker for confidence.

I forced a laugh. "Sorry. I smell books."

"You shouldn't apologize," he said. "Girls apologize too much."

"Oh." I was startled. "Um. Sorry?"

He laughed, not kindly.

I knew I apologized too much, truth be told. It was

something Cecile had often called me on. We apologize when we've done nothing wrong! she'd say, pounding a fist on the table for emphasis. Women go out of our way to make ourselves the bad guy, to make men feel like nothing is ever their fault, when actually most things are men's fault! I was a feminist too, in my heart, but I wasn't as loud about it as Cecile. I wasn't as loud about anything as Cecile. Few people were.

I regrouped. I shouldn't apologize for smelling a book. Who was it hurting, anyway? "I like to smell them," I told the linebacker.

"Do they smell sweet?"

"You've never smelled a book?"

He raised his eyebrows.

I held one out to him. "Try it."

The linebacker reached out and closed his hand around my book. Suddenly, weirdly, I found myself reluctant to let it go. I forced myself to release it. He lifted it to his face and held it there for a moment. "Very nice," he said, his gaze locked on mine.

He hadn't inhaled.

He hadn't smelled it.

"Do you go to Adams High?" I asked.

He hesitated, then shook his head. "I don't live here."

"You're from out of town? Where?"

"Do you always ask so many questions?"

"I'm a friendly person."

"What's your name, friendly person?"

"Rena." The moment I said it I felt as if I'd lost

something, given up some important information. Why was I feeling so strange today? "I'm Rena."

He nodded slowly, as if I was confirming something he'd already suspected.

"And you are?" I prompted. This guy had no conception of social niceties.

"Bristol," he said.

"That's your name or where you're from?" I didn't hear an accent, but you never know.

"My name," he said.

"That's an interesting name," I tried. "Is it a family name?"

He stepped close to me. "You shouldn't ask so many questions."

I felt about an inch high, but I summoned what dignity I could and reached out for the book. "I should go check out." God, now I was going to let this guy chase me out of the store? I had nowhere to go until Cecile picked me up.

He stared at me for a long moment. It seemed to drag on and on. I wanted to look away, but somehow, I couldn't break his gaze. I felt almost naked, as if he was making an in-depth study of me against my will, pulling out all my flaws and secrets.

Finally, he looked away and tossed me the book as if it was nothing. "As you like."

I backed away, then turned and almost ran to the front of the store. I could feel his eyes boring into my back the whole way, and I expected to feel his hand on my shoulder spinning me around or hear his voice at close range telling me again what I shouldn't do. I even looked back once. He was just standing there, still leaning against the shelf, watching me go.

So creepy.

I dumped all four books in my arms onto the counter—so much for limiting myself—and pulled out my phone while Ms. Kate rang me up. Ready to go, I typed. pick me up at sol's coffee?

Cecile's reply came a beat later. DON'T DRINK COFFEE!

I loved that girl. Just water and scone. promise

Be right there

Ms. Kate handed me a bag with my purchases. "You have a blessed day now, Rena."

"You too." I hurried out of the store before she could ask me to sit down for coffee again, before creepy Bristol could change his mind about letting me go without protest. No more weird strangers, I thought as I pushed through the door. Just me, my new books, and a scone to nibble on. A perfect afternoon.

Then I crashed headlong into a guy and fell down.

"Oh, pardon me" he said, holding out a hand to help me up.

I waved his hand away and got to my feet. "I'm all right." I wasn't, entirely—my butt was going to have a nice bruise later—but I'd be damned if I was going to start discussing my butt with this random person.

"I apologize," he said, brushing his light brown hair out

of his eyes. "I must watch where I'm going."

"No, its fine, I was rushing." I glanced at my phone. I should still be rushing, really, if I wanted to make it to Sol's and have a chance to get my scone before Cecile arrived. "Excuse me, I'm meeting a friend."

"You are?" He looked around.

"She isn't here yet. I'm going to wait for her over there." There I went again, telling every boy I ran into every little thing about me. Next, I'd be disclosing my bra size.

The guy frowned. "But you can't wait alone. It isn't safe."

At that I had to laugh. "I'm going to sit in a coffeehouse. What isn't safe?"

"There could be dangerous people around," he said, very seriously, and for a moment he seemed to be glancing in the bookstore window. It was almost as if he guessed what had just happened to me, that I'd just come across someone strange.

Stranger than this guy, though?

Relax, I ordered myself. He's not a Bristol. He's not being creepy. Except he definitely was, a little bit. He too was standing too close to me, looking at me searchingly as if trying to divine something about me without bothering to ask.

"I'll wait with you," he said. "Until your friend arrives."

I stepped back. "That isn't necessary."

"You don't have to speak to me," he said. "Just let me accompany you to the coffee shop. I'll even take a different table if that would make you more comfortable."

"Well…" I was being ridiculous, but after what I had been through in the bookstore; it had put me on high alert. Although the guy standing in front of me wasn't nearly as eerie as Bristol. "That's okay. I mean, you could sit at my table if you want."

"Very well."

"I'm only having a scone."

"I would love to join you for a scone."

"You're a little strange," I chanced with a raise of my brow. "Did you know?'

Much to my relief, he smiled. "I did, actually."

"Let me guess. You don't live around here?'

"No," he agreed. "I don't live around here."

"I'm Rena."

"Hello, Rena," he said. "My name is Cryder."

"Cryder," I repeated. I restrained myself—barely—from asking if it was a family name.

We started the walk to Sol's.

Suddenly, Cecile's car pulled up like a bat out of hell, nearly making me jump a foot in the air. I knew — or at least I'd always suspected — she drove that thing like a crazy person when I wasn't with her. I frowned at her. We were going to have a serious talk later about the merits of defensive driving.

"Hey, girl," she said. "Get in."

I looked apologetically at Cryder. "This is my friend. Cecile. Cecile, this is Cryder."

"Cryder?' Now Cecile was raising an eyebrow. "That's a name?'

"Yes," Cryder said mildly.

"I didn't get my scone," I told Cecile.

"Well, we'll pick up McDonald's or something. I have to get home. Jack from World Studies is going to call me about the homework, and you know I can't answer the phone while I'm driving."

I did know, and I appreciated it. "I'm sorry," I told Cryder. "I have to go. It was nice meeting you."

"Very nice meeting you also, Rena."

I got in Cecile's car.

"Who was that guy?' she asked as we pulled away from the curb.

"I don't know," I admitted. "Just...some guy."

"He was a little weird."

I glanced over my shoulder. Cryder was still standing there, just as Bristol had been, staring after me as I left. That look he was wearing sent a bit of a shiver down my spine.

I turned in my seat and faced the road ahead. "You have no idea."

Chapter Four

CECILE ALWAYS SLEPT IN ON SATURDAYS. I could never do it — my body was just too accustomed to getting up at the same time each day, I guess, and anyway, I'd always been a light sleeper. I enjoyed the quiet hours I had to myself, though. More than any other time, Saturday mornings made me feel as if I were truly at home in a place that belonged to me instead of a guest in someone else's house.

I rolled out of bed and padded down to the kitchen. It was nine AM and Cecile wasn't likely to stir until at least noon. Mr. and Mrs. Danvers always went to the farmers' market together for several hours on Saturdays, so I had the place to myself for the time being. I poured out a bowl of Cinnamon Toast Crunch, slopped some milk over it, and took it into the living room to see what was on TV. The Danvers' corgi, Baxter, hopped up on the couch beside me and nosed my hand until I gave him a piece of cereal. "Good boy, Bax."

I settled on a tennis match, the mindless rhythm of the ball whacking against rackets and courts proving the perfect background noise as I went through my morning Internet routine. Emails first—mostly junk, but one note from Mrs. Dawson saying she hoped I was feeling better. I hit reply on that one and typed out a quick I'm doing much better today, thanks for your concern! I hit send before I had time to make myself feel too awkward about emailing a teacher. After all, she wouldn't have asked if she didn't want to know.

I went to Instagram next. There were a few new likes on a selfie from last weekend of me and Cecile sharing a banana split. It was one of the more popular pictures on my account, either because of Cecile or because of the ice cream. Everyone I knew loved Cecile and ice cream.

On my Facebook news feed, a stupid meme was going around. Most people won't post this, but those that do are true friends! I definitely wasn't going to post it. Talk about manipulative.

New friend request, my screen informed me with a little red notification.

Weird—I was already friends with everyone at school. I clicked the request. Cryder Conti, it read. The picture wasn't a face, just a photo of what looked like a barren tree. Who?

The memory came rushing back. How could I forget the guy with the weird name and weird mannerisms I'd met outside Book City? He'd certainly left an impression. But how had he found me?

Reminding myself that I could always block him later if this got creepy, I hit accept on the request. A moment later, a chat window popped up. He was online.

Good morning, Rena.

With a sense that I'd stepped into something surreal, I typed back good morning.

How are you today?

Fine. How'd you find my facebook? Well that sounded stupid. Like my Facebook was some big state secret?

Rena isn't a common name, the message came back. And your picture confirmed it was you.

I glanced at my picture. It was one of the few I have where Cecile isn't pictured too. It was from last Halloween, and I was wearing so much makeup that I couldn't believe this picture was all he'd had to confirm my identity. I wouldn't have expected someone who knew me well to be absolutely sure who they were looking at in that photo.

He must have really been paying attention to me yesterday. I wasn't sure if that was flattering or creepy. Then again, I wasn't sure if Cryder himself was flattering or creepy.

what are you up to? I typed, realizing I wasn't holding up my end of the conversation.

Wondering if you'd like to go get that scone with me this evening.

* * *

"You should definitely go," Cecile said. "You need a little fun."

"I can't take you seriously while you're doing that." She was lying chest-down on her bedroom floor, back arched up so her butt was over her head and her toes touched the ground on either side of her face. I sat cross-legged?on her bed, computer in hand, staring at Cryder's still-unanswered Facebook message. I was so freaked out by the situation that I'd had to wake Cecile and fill her in. I should have known her advice would be to leap in with both feet.

Cecile rolled down out of her yoga pose and stretched into Downward Facing Dog, butt high in the air. "When was the last time you went on a date, Rena?'

"Homecoming." Brett Troyer. We'd gone as friends.

She shifted her weight to lift a hand and wave it dismissively at me. "Doesn't count."

"Why doesn't it count!?'

"Did you kiss him?'

"Brett? Of course not."

"So."

"So what, you want me to kiss this person? I've spoken to him for all of five minutes, Cecile."

She stood upright and stretched her arms back over her head. "That's why you go on the date. Get to know him and find out if you want to kiss him."

"I don't know about this."

"Go on. It would be good for you." She shook out her limbs and came over to sit beside me on the bed. "You never have any fun, Rena."

"I have fun!"

"No, okay, I know you do, but you always have the same kind of fun. You need to get out of your comfort zone."

"Why do I need to do that? I like my comfort zone. It's comfortable!"

She laughed. "Do it for me. If you don't have fun, I'll bake you apple tartlets to make up for it."

I could hardly say no to that. "You promise?"

"Scout's honor!"

With a deep breath, I turned back to the Facebook conversation. How's five o'clock?

The reply was immediate as though he was waiting on my response. Perfect. I'll pick you up.

* * *

The doorbell rang promptly as the digital clock over the oven clicked to 5:00. "He's here!" Cecile sang out, dropping the mascara wand she'd been using to put 'finishing touches' on my look. — "We're just grabbing coffee," I'd told her. She'd rolled her eyes somewhat smugly and said, "you never know, though!" —

I scooted off my stool, waving a hand at Cecile to quiet her, and opened the door. There stood Cryder, a massive bouquet of flowers in his arms. His light brown hair, which I remembered being in disarray when we'd first met, was now combed neatly and parted to the right. He wore pressed slacks, shined shoes, and a blazer and bow tie. Thank God I'd taken Cecile's advice and put on a sundress instead of the jeans and t-shirt I'd wanted to wear.

Cecile came up behind me. "Nice bow tie." She took

the flowers out of his hands. "I'll pop these in a vase for you, Rena."

"Thank you," Cryder said, with no apparent trace of humor. "It was my grandfather's." He turned to me. "Rena, I thought perhaps we could begin the evening with dinner?"

"I only have money for coffee."

"This would be my treat."

"She'd be delighted," Cecile cut off my objections. "Rena, just remember that Mom wants you home by midnight, okay?"

"I'll have her back in plenty of time," Cryder assured Cecile.

"Excuse me," I said, annoyed. "I am standing right here, you know."

"Of course, you are," Cryder held out his arm to me. "Shall we?"

His gaze locked with mine, and I felt my irritation dissipate like fog. He was so odd, but so oddly charming. Showing up here with those flowers, dressed so smartly...he was a real gentleman, not anything like the boys I knew at school. I let him take my arm and lead me out the front door.

All through dinner, I was barely able to swallow a bite. Cryder had chosen one of my favorite Italian restaurants, but my head was so packed with questions that it was all I could do to keep from interrogating him over breadsticks. He didn't seem that hungry either — when his plate of spaghetti was delivered, he set about cutting it into bite-size pieces and nibbling at them methodically. I'd never seen anyone cut their pasta into a grid before. Didn't everyone just twirl it up on their fork, the way I always had? One more question for the growing pile.

Cryder dabbed his mouth with his napkin. "You haven't eaten much," he said, indicating the lasagna on my plate. "Was it not good?"

"No, it's fine."

"Because we can have it sent back to the kitchen."

"No, no. I guess…I guess I'm just nervous," I admitted.

A smile cracked Cryder's face. "So am I."

"Really?" A knot of tension I hadn't been aware of suddenly loosened in my chest. His confession put us back on even ground, somehow, even though there was still so much I didn't know about him.

"Why don't we get out of here and take a walk," he suggested.

"Sounds perfect."

Cryder flagged a waiter and paid the bill — cash, I noticed, who carried that much cash around anymore? — and we headed out into the dimming light. After a brief stop at the coffee shop next door for iced lattes, we turned our steps toward Palermo Park.

"So why did you decide to find me on Facebook?" I asked. The change in setting, walking side by side instead of facing each other in the mood lighting of the restaurant, had made it easier to talk, somehow.

"I wanted to see you again," he said.

"Just based on one chance meeting, though?"

"I don't really believe in chance meetings."

"How can you not believe in chance meetings? What else do you call it?'

"Fate."

"You think we were fated to meet outside Book City?'

He squinted at me. "You don't believe in fate."

"I guess I just find it hard to believe the universe cares what happens to me on a day-to-day basis."

"Why not?' We'd arrived at the park, and he took my hand and led me to a bench under a boxelder maple. "Do you think of yourself as someone who could be overlooked?'

I swallowed hard. The truth, though I didn't want to admit it on a date, was that if I accepted fate as a reality, I would have to acknowledge that I'd been fated to lose my parents in the awful way I had. I couldn't stand to let myself believe that was something the universe wanted for me. Ever since they'd died, I'd felt repulsed by any suggestion of an organizing principle to the universe, be it fate, religion, or karma. Sometimes terrible things just happened for no reason at all. It was the only way I could make sense of it.

I forced the unpleasant memories out of my head. What kind of girl thinks about death when a cute guy is rubbing his thumb along the back of her hand and staring at her like she's a work of art? "You found me on Facebook because it was fate that we met?'

"Yes," he said softly, leaning in, his face now only inches from mine. "Because we're meant to know each other."

I felt breathless, mesmerized. "But how can you be so

sure?"

"You tell me," he whispered, and closed the distance between us.

The moment his lips met mine, I was transported. A slight moan escaped my throat, but it was as if I was very far away from the sound, lost deep in his embrace. It wasn't my first kiss —there had been boys from school; nothing serious, the odd afternoon make-out session. But in those instances, I'd always felt detached, half of me plotting my escape even as the guy in question groped for the hem of my shirt. This was utterly different. I was immersed in Cryder, in the warm press of his mouth against mine, the tingles of excitement that shot down my spine every time he moved. One of his hands was threaded in my hair, a thing I'd never allowed because guys always found a way to accidentally pull at loose strands. I couldn't even bring myself to worry about that this time. His other hand rested on my lower back, holding me to him. I waited, but he didn't try to slip under my shirt. I probably would have let him, too. What an amazing turn of luck to be on a date with such a gentleman!

Maybe it was fate.

Whatever it was, I was more than happy for it to continue. Cryder cupped my head and tipped me back, deepening the kiss, and I wondered—are we going to lie down? I wouldn't have minded. We were in a public place, on a hard bench, on a first date, and if this boy wanted to lie on top of me and kiss me, I was going to allow it.

He didn't, though. The gentlemanly behavior

continued. He held me up so I was lying in his arms. I wrapped one arm around his shoulders to secure myself and, blissfully, let the other trail off the side of the bench to graze the ground. I had never been kissed this way before in my life.

Dimly, I registered my fingers trailing in something warm and wet. Mud? I must have made a noise, because Cryder pulled away. "Is everything all right, Rena?"

"I'm fine, it's just —" I lifted my hand to show him, my other arm already pulling him back to me, annoyed at the interruption.

And then I blinked.

The liquid on my hand wasn't mud. It was thick, red, and tacky.

Cryder's eyes flew wide and he pushed me away from him so hard it bordered on violent. "Rena."

"Wh-what?"

"Get up. Let's go."

Frowning, I looked down. There was a pool of red on the dirt beside our bench.

"Rena!" Cryder snapped. "Don't!"

I leaned over.

And screamed.

Lying under the bench, facedown, was the body of a man with blood coming from a gaping neck wound. Though his eyes were open, they were utterly empty, and his lips and fingers were blue. He was dead.

Chapter Five

"RENA. RENA!"

Cryder's voice was a growl, blending with the car's engine as we sped through the streets. I came back to myself abruptly, aware that it was the third or fourth time since he'd whisked me out of the park. He kept calling my name, calling me back. I kept drifting away.

"Rena!"

"W-we have to call the police." My teeth chattered as a tremor ran through my body. Cryder made a displeased grunt and did something to the heat. Maybe it would make a difference. I didn't know. My hand—the one that I'd trailed in the ground (in the blood)—felt contaminated, disgusting, appalling. I wanted to plunge it into boiling water. I held it as far from my body as I could, behind the seat, reaching into the back of the car like if I didn't have to see it it wouldn't have to belong to me.

"Stay with me," Cryder said, and took the next corner without slowing down, throwing me sideways into the door of the car. I wanted to scream. Slow down. Slow down. I couldn't get the words out.

"Cryder, we have to call the cops."

He shook his head. "We need to get you home."

I fumbled for my phone, reaching across myself with my uncontaminated hand to fish it from the opposite pocket of my dress. "Kids play in that park."

"Someone else will find it."

"I'm calling 911."

"Rena, just hold on, okay? Wait until we get home, I'll do it for you. Take a deep breath, you're hyperventilating."

Of course I am. I touched a dead body. This car is going to crash.

"Close your eyes," Cryder said.

"I can't." What, and not watch the road?

"Okay, then look at…" He paused, and I became aware of the fact that my gaze was flitting around like a butterfly on speed. "Look at this," he said finally, removing a hand from the steering wheel to touch the air freshener hanging from his rearview mirror.

"Keep your hands on the wheel, all right?"

I expected an argument—Cecile always argued when I tried to correct her driving, and she knew why I was anxious about it—but Cryder just nodded and returned his hand to the two-o-clock position. Grateful, I forced myself to fix my eyes on the air freshener.

"Breathe in," Cryder said. "Count to four."

I did.

"Hold it for six," he said. "Now exhale for eight."

I breathed out. I only made it to a count of five, but Cryder nodded. "That's good. Better. Keep doing that, okay?'

"'Kay," I huffed out, breathing.

By the time Cryder turned onto Cecile's street, I was surprised to find that the technique had kind of worked. I didn't feel calm, exactly, and I still wanted to scour the skin from my hand, but the dead man's face wasn't flashing before my eyes every time I blinked anymore. I didn't feel like I was slipping in and out of conscious thought. "How did you know that breathing thing?' I asked Cryder.

"Just something I picked up." He parked the car. "Let's get you inside, okay?'

I registered with some surprise, but less alarm than I would have expected, the fact that he was inviting himself in. Leaving for our date, I'd been unsure exactly how I wanted it to end—would he try to kiss me when he dropped me off, and if he did try, would I let him? It was a strange thought now after the intensity of our connection in the park, but that, too, had come out of nowhere, and if it hadn't been for what happened next, it would have been the most surprising thing I could have imagined. As things stood, I was glad to have Cryder's hand on my elbow, escorting me to the door. I was glad he was going to stay with me. I didn't want to walk in there alone and explain to Cecile and her parents what had happened, what I'd seen. They'd think I was crazy.

I had a key to the house, of course, but Cryder rang the doorbell before I could reach for it. Through the door came the familiar beat of socked feet running down the stairs and across the floorboards, and I leaned heavily into Cryder. A moment later, Cecile threw open the door.

"Rena! You're back already? Curfew isn't until…" She stopped, took in my face. "Are you okay?"

"Can we come in?" Cryder asked. It was strange that he was asking permission to bring me in—I did live here, after all—but a part of me liked it. He was tying the two of us together, in a way, including me in his own need for Cecile's consent.

"Of course," Cecile said. "Should I get Mom? She's in the basement."

"No, don't," I said. Maybe I'd have to before this was over, but right now the last thing I wanted was to explain the situation to Mrs. Danvers. "I'm going to wash my hands. Just keep quiet and head upstairs."

"I'll come with you." She glanced at Cryder. "Make yourself at home. There are sodas in the fridge."

"Thank you." Cryder settled on the couch.

The Danvers' downstairs bathroom was small, just big enough for a wedged-in toilet opposite a sink, and Cecile had to perch on the toilet tank with her feet propped on the lid to make room for both of us to be in there at the same time. I rested my hand in the sink like it was an object and started the hot water running, waiting for it to warm up.

"What's going on?" Cecile asked. "Should I make him leave? He didn't try anything, did he?"

"Try anything?" My mind was mired in thoughts of

death, and for a moment I didn't understand what she was asking. "Oh. No. We kissed."

"Well that's..." I could feel her puzzled frown. "Good? Right?"

"Yeah."

"So, what's wrong? You look terrible."

I leaned forward, bracing my forehead against the mirror, and held my hand under the water. The heat was painful, but when I closed my eyes, I could envision sheets of blood running off my skin, impurities washing away down the drain. "Someone died."

"What?"

"At the park."

"What do you mean? Like an accident? What happened?"

"I don't know, I...it didn't seem like an accident, Cecile."

"I don't understand. Tell me what happened."

"There was a body. Under the bench by the tree. It looked...I don't know. Mauled or stabbed or something. It looked like somebody put it there." A shudder wracked its way down my spine and suddenly I was gagging.

"Whoa, okay." Behind me, Cecile slid her arms undermine, holding me up, and I spat into the sink. "It's all right. You're okay? Nobody hurt you?"

"Nobody hurt me."

"And you didn't actually see this happen? Just the..."

"Just the body."

"Holy shit."

"I know."

"What do we do?"

"We call the police, right? That's what you do when you…" I swallowed hard. "When you witness a crime."

"You didn't actually witness the crime, though. Right?"

"Does it matter? I saw the body!"

"No, I'm just saying…you should calm down first, right? Make sure you know what you're going to say? Because if you call the police to report a murder…"

"You think it was murder?"

"I don't know." She met my eyes. "I don't think there are any wild animals in Palermo Park."

"But maybe…"

"Rena, I don't think anyone, but a human could put someone under a bench after they'd died. That sounds really deliberate."

"But why would anybody do that?" I asked. "If you'd, you know, killed somebody, why would you leave them out in the open? Isn't that asking to get caught? Wouldn't it be really easy for someone to have seen what happened, how it got there? And it's probably covered with DNA, right?"

"I don't know." She bit her lip. "You're right. We need to call the police."

"Cryder said he was going to. We should talk to him. Make sure he mentions all this stuff."

Cecile nodded. "Are you ready to go back out there?"

I took a deep breath. "I'm ready."

"Hey." She hugged me. "I'm here, okay?"

"Thanks, Cecile." She really was the best friend anyone could ask for.

She threaded her fingers through mine and led the way out of the bathroom and back to the living room. I was momentarily shocked to see that Cryder was gone, but a split second later I heard his voice. "In the park. That's right."

Cecile raised her eyebrows and pointed toward the window. Cryder had gone out to the porch. The two of us crossed to the couch and sat quietly by unspoken agreement, listening.

"No, I don't think so," Cryder said. "I didn't even notice it at first."

Cecile squeezed my hand. "See?' she whispered. "It's under control. The cops know what to do."

I nodded.

"I shouldn't even be here," Cryder said.

Cecile frowned at me. I shrugged.

"He's here, Drake. He wants Rena."

What the hell? Cecile mouthed at me.

I was tense now, and my heart was pounding. What is he saying? Cryder had promised to call the police, but he was clearly speaking to someone else now. Had he already reported what we'd seen? Or had he lied when he told me he was going to? Who on Earth was Drake? And what did Cryder mean by he wants Rena? Who wanted me?

The murderer?

My blood turned to ice. Cecile reached out and

squeezed my trembling hand.

Moments later, the front door opened and Cryder came back in. He paused in the doorway when he saw us staring at him. "Is everything all right?"

"Who were you on the phone with?" I was expecting my voice to waver, but it came out steady, and I felt momentarily proud of myself and even pleased before I remembered that I might be a murderer's next target, that the boy I liked (did I like him? Oh, God, how could that question even still fit in my mind after everything that had happened today?) might be lying to me.

"I wasn't on the phone," Cryder said. "I was just getting some air."

"We heard you," Cecile snapped.

Cryder sighed. "It's complicated. I'm sorry."

"You're sorry? We heard you say Rena's name. We heard you say that someone wanted her. Who wants her? For what?"

Cryder, to his credit, looked deeply uncomfortable. I could understand. I'd been on the receiving end of one of Cecile's interrogations myself once or twice. "I can't explain right now, I'm sorry." He turned to me. "Rena, I need you to trust me."

"Trust you?" Cecile snorted with derision. "Why would she trust you? You're blatantly lying to us. We don't even know who you are."

"I know." Cryder ran a hand through his hair, raking it out of position and into the mess it had been when I'd first met him. To my shock, I felt a sudden tug of attraction. What was wrong with me? How could I be so drawn to this person when I knew for a fact he was lying to me, when I suspected he might even be putting me in danger? No wonder Cecile was so angry. If our positions were reversed, I'd have thrown Cryder out of the house by now.

Somehow, though, I couldn't quite bring myself to do it.

"I don't know if I can trust you," I said to Cryder.

"You can't," Cecile said.

"But I want to."

The look of relief that crossed his face made me want to get to my feet and put my arms around him. And that impulse made me want to lock myself in my room and ban myself from dating until I grew some common sense.

"I have some things to take care of," Cryder said, turning toward the door. "Rena, don't go anywhere alone, okay?" He glanced at Cecile. "Stay with her."

"Obviously," Cecile said, in the same tone she used when I reminded her to use her turn signal.

"I'll see you again soon, Rena." He paused. "Thank you for the date. I truly enjoyed most of it. I hope you did too."

Chapter Six

THE DOOR BANGED SHUT BEHIND CRYDER. I sat frozen on the couch, my hands pressed tight between my knees, struggling to make sense of everything that had happened in the past hour. The cold dead body in the park (Oh God, don't think about that now I wanted to jump up and wash my hand again), speeding home so fast I was absolutely sure we were going to end up in a wreck and die, and Cryder making a mysterious phone call on the porch, admitting he had lied to us but refusing to explain himself.

Me, saying I wanted to trust him.

Why on Earth had I said that?

I barely knew him. Today was only the second time we'd ever met, and the first time hardly counted, running into each other on the sidewalk outside Book City. I'd let him feed me that line about fate, for God's sake—what kind of garbage was that? Who was I? Who was he?

"He could be the murderer, you know." Cecile's thoughts were apparently on the same track as mine.

"He's not the murderer," I said.

"It would make sense." Cecile paced in front of me, her hands on her hips. "He's the one who took you to the park. He's the one who said he was going to call the cops and didn't."

"What, he brought me to the scene of the crime on purpose? Why would anyone do that?"

"Don't ask me to explain how a murderer's mind works." She pulled back the window curtain. "God, he's just lurking out there. He's not even leaving."

"What?" I spun around and peeked out. There he was, leaning against his car, the phone pressed to his ear. "What is he doing?"

"We should call the police," Cecile said. "This is messed up, Rena."

"I'm going to find out what's going on." I stood up.

She grabbed my wrist. "Are you insane? Don't go out there!"

"He's not a murderer, Cecile."

"You don't know that!"

I shook her hand off. "Come out with me, then. You can bring your phone and call 911 if anything happens."

"This is a bad idea." But I was already moving, so she snatched up her phone from the end table, following me out the door and into the yard.

Cryder darted his head up like a bird when the front door shut behind us. His hyper-alert stance made him look nervous, guilty, and for a moment I wondered if Cecile had a point. Then I shook it off. Cryder was acting suspicious, sure, but he couldn't have killed the man in the park. It just didn't make any logical sense. He'd been with me for an hour before we'd even gone there, and there was no way the dead body had been lying under that bench for a whole hour in the middle of Palermo Park and no one had seen it. It had to have been put there right before we arrived. Nothing else made any sense.

I marched over to Cryder. "Hang up the phone," I said. "I want to talk to you."

He held up a finger and turned away. "Look, I'll call you back in a minute," He muttered. "I need to handle the situation here first." He paused. "I thought I had, too. She's smart, okay? Just let me...yeah. I'll call you back."

He turned back to me and put the phone in his pocket. "Rena, I know this is a lot to process."

"A lot to process?'

"You said you wanted to trust me," he said, his voice soft. I couldn't tell if he was trying to cut Cecile out of our conversation by keeping things quiet, or if this was just some kind of tonal attempt at keeping me calm. Either way, it wasn't going to work.

"You were on the phone with the same person as before, weren't you?' I demanded.

"Rena, calm down."

"Don't tell me to calm down! That's such a guy thing to say!"

"What?'

"Why should I be calm when someone's dead, Cryder?'

"I need you to trust me."

"I don't even know you!"

"Rena." He moved toward me.

Suddenly I was seeing spots. The ground tilted alarmingly beneath my feet. Gravity—usually so reliable—was pulling me forward instead of down, and I was sinking, melting slowly through the air, into the earth, which was far too close…

"Rena!"

Cecile's voice cut the fog around my brain like a knife. Someone's strong arms were holding me up, resting me against the bulk of a torso. Cryder. "Help me get her inside," he said, his voice coming from very far away.

"What happened?' That was Cecile again. She sounded near tears, and I wanted to respond, to tell her I'm fine, but I couldn't make my lips move. I felt utterly weak in the way I sometimes did seconds after waking up, before my body remembered how to be alert. Why couldn't I pull myself out of this daze?

God, this was just like after my parents…

No. Stop. This isn't that.

A moment later, my body settled against the couch cushions. Cryder's face swam into focus above me, then back out. "Rena, drink this, okay?'

"Mm?' Drink what?

I felt the rim of a thermos pressed to my lips; lukewarm liquid spilled into my mouth. I swallowed reflexively. The taste was unfamiliar, heavy and nutritious. Vegetable juice? I wanted to ask, but it was too hard, so I moved my hand against Cryder's wrist and hoped he'd understand I was saying thank you.

"More," he said, and offered the drink again. This time I was prepared and took a longer swallow. I could actually feel strength returning as it flowed down my throat and toward my muscles. Whatever this was, Cryder ought to patent it.

He wrapped his arm behind my shoulders and gave me slow sips, and I let him. I let myself forget my anger and suspicion. In my gut, I realized, I did trust him. I had to trust my instincts, didn't I? If I couldn't trust myself, what did I have? Besides, I could feel the drink he was giving me making me stronger, helping me recover, and if he wasn't looking out for my best interests, why would he bother with that?

Cryder pulled the thermos away. I must have whined in protest, because he pressed a finger to my lips. "Enough for now," he said. "That's good. Take it slow."

I blinked my eyes open. My vision was clear now. Cryder was leaning over me, smiling. "Are you all right?" he asked, tracing his thumb under my lower lip, and I felt a drop of liquid wipe away.

"I think so." I began to sit up.

He placed a firm hand on my shoulder. "Stay down for now. Make sure you're steady first. That might take a while to work."

"What did you give me?"

"Yeah." Cecile's voice came from somewhere behind him, absolutely spitting fire. "What did you give her?"

Cryder sat back on his heels. Some quiet, insistent part of me wanted to grab him and pull him back to me, but I resisted. "I can explain," he said.

Cecile crossed her arms over her chest. "Good. Do."

"Rena hasn't been well lately," he said. "Maybe you've noticed. Dizzy spells? Maybe passing out, and you haven't been able to pinpoint the cause?'

"There's nothing wrong with her," Cecile snapped.

But I wasn't so sure. Suddenly I remembered my unsteadiness the day I'd first met Cryder. The fact that I'd nearly passed out in the school parking lot, and then again in class. And there was that voice I'd thought I'd heard...could that have been a hallucination? Was something really wrong with me? I thought back to a few years ago, when Cecile and I had been obsessed with Grey's Anatomy, and how unexplained dizziness and hallucinations were almost always harbingers of brain tumors or cancer and horrible death. What's wrong with me?

Cryder's hand settled on top of mine. "She'll be all right," he said. "She just needs the proper vitamins in her diet, and she'll be just fine."

"What the hell are you talking about?' Cecile demanded. "How could you possibly know any of that? You aren't her doctor. Or have you been watching her?'

Cryder's eyes went wide for a quick flash before returning to normal, and with a calm voice he responded, "My father's a doctor."

"Your father's never even met Rena, and is there a

reason you didn't answer my questions?" She turned to me. "You can't possibly be buying this."

"I don't know," I hedged. After all, I was experiencing some unsettling symptoms, and whatever was in his thermos had made me feel better. I'd much rather think that whatever was going on could be easily managed with a protein shake, or whatever that was.

"I want to know what's in the thermos," Cecile said.

"It's a nutrient blend my family makes," Cryder said. "As long as she has some every day, her condition won't deteriorate."

"This is insane. You're insane." Cecile tugged at the end of her ponytail. "I'm calling my mom."

Cryder sighed. "Wait."

"I knew it. I knew you were sketchy."

"I'll call the police," he said. "Will that convince you?"

"Why would I believe you? You've done nothing but lie!"

"Because I'll do it right here where you can listen, okay? I'll call them and report what we saw in the park, and you can listen, and then we'll talk about Rena." He lowered his voice, and I wondered if maybe now it was me he didn't want to hear. "I care about her."

"She's my family."

"I know that. I know you care for her too. I'm asking you to help me."

Cecile hesitated. Then she pressed her lips together. "Call the police."

I closed my eyes and let their voices wash over me as they made the phone call. Much as I didn't want to believe it, I thought Cryder might know what he was talking about. I had felt different lately. I wished I could have more of the strange drink right now—I craved the strength it seemed to give me. I still didn't feel fully recovered from my dizzy spell. I faded in and out of full awareness, lulled by the sound of Cryder reporting our experience to the police, and let myself drift in the fantasy that he was telling a scary story, that all of it had happened to someone else. It didn't go with Mrs. Danvers' plush sofa cushions, with the familiar cast of the environmentally-friendly light bulbs Cecile insisted on. It didn't go with me.

At some point, without my full awareness, the phone call ended. Cryder and Cecile were talking now, talking like they didn't hate each other. They sounded like cautious allies. "She has been different," Cecile said, a note of fear in her voice, and I longed to reassure her that everything would be okay. As soon as I woke up, I would do that.

"I knew from the moment I met her," Cryder said.

"Is that why you wanted to take her out? Was it all a ruse to evaluate her health?"

"The date was real," he said. "My...feelings. Are real."

"I still don't trust you."

"That's okay."

"And it's really just a vitamin drink?"

"You just saw her drink some," he pointed out. "If I was poisoning her, you'd see some sort of ill effect."

Cecile frowned. "I suppose that's true, but let me sniff it or see what's in there." Her hand was out, waiting for the thermos.

"You can sniff it all you want." Cryder handed over the thermos, his eyes glued on Cecile as he spoke. "You don't have to believe me about the rest of it. Just...please, see that she gets some of this every day. If she doesn't, things will get worse for her."

"What will happen?"

"I can't say, exactly."

Cecile blew out a frustrated puff of air. "This would be a lot easier if you could say, you know."

"Yes, I realize that."

"I'll do it. I will."

"Thank you." I could hear the relief in his voice. "You don't know how much that means to me."

"Oh, don't flatter yourself. I'm not doing it for you."

"Nevertheless."

"Can you show yourself out? I think Rena and I need some time."

"Of course."

A pause. Then, "Does she have a phone number where she can reach you?"

"Here." The sound of pen scratching on paper. "Call any time."

Chapter Seven

"DO YOU THINK I SHOULD BE DRINKING IT, too?" Cecile rolled Cryder's thermos back and forth between her hands. "I mean, if it's such a powerful vitamin, maybe…"

"Trust me, you don't want to." I closed my eyes and threw back my spiked orange juice like a shot, trying not to grimace as I swallowed it. "It makes everything taste like crap."

"Really?" She spun open the lid to the thermos and took a deep inhale. "It doesn't smell that bad."

"I'm not even totally convinced I should be drinking it. We don't know what it is."

"He said vitamin."

"Right, and I'm sure it's FDA-approved."

"You feel better though, right?'

I had to admit that I did. Cecile had been adding Cryder's mystery supplement to everything I drank for a week now, and I actually couldn't remember when I'd felt healthier. Not only had I had less dizzy spells, but I'd also been sleeping better, waking up more easily, and feeling more energetic all day long. Whatever was in the thermos, I could no longer deny that it was having some kind of positive effect.

Which didn't make me feel that much better about my situation. What was wrong with me? What kind of illness could be so easily cured, not by doctors or medicine, but by a foul-tasting concoction that I wasn't even allowed to know the ingredients of? And how had Cryder known after seeing me pass out one time that this was what I needed?

"He seemed like he was expecting it," Cecile had said when I asked her. "Like he knew all along that you were sick, or whatever, and he was just waiting for some kind of evidence. Once he found it, he could give us the drink."

"You're saying he knew when he asked me out?"

"I mean, who brings a thermos of spooky vitamin juice on a date, right? He must have known."

Well, that was even creepier.

That night I'd called Cryder to try to get better answers out of him, but he'd been as vague as ever. "I'm really sorry," he'd said, sounding as if he truly meant it. "I just can't explain it. Not yet."

Near tears with frustration, I had to swallow three times hard before answering. "Cryder, this is unreasonable."

"I know. I understand."

"Maybe I should just go see a doctor." This was my trump card. Surely if I threatened to cut him off, to stop doing what he wanted, he would have to give me answers. He didn't need to know that I had no plans to give up his drink. How could I, when it made me feel so alive?

"If that's what you think is best," Cryder had said.

Damn it.

Now, watching Cecile fidget with the thermos, trying to force the vile drink (whatever it was, it did not mix well with orange juice) down my throat, I realized that if I wanted answers, I would have to find a way to get them on my own. "Cecile?"

"Yeah?"

"Plans today?"

"Not yet. Why? Do you want to watch that Vietnam War documentary?"

"I told you I didn't want to watch that. It's depressing. No, I was wondering if you'd go somewhere with me."

"Where?"

"Well...to drive around, I guess."

She stopped rolling the thermos. "What, just around? Not to anywhere?" She raised an eyebrow.

"I mean..." God, this was going to sound crazy, wasn't it. "I thought we could try to find out what Cryder's up to."

"What do you mean?"

"I mean follow him."

"You want to stalk Cryder?"

I sighed. "I don't know if I do, but I feel like we should, to get answers."

"He is a bit on the scary side."

I nodded. "He's bizarre. He shows up out of nowhere, asks me out after bumping into me on the street once, then on our very first date he's packing this wonder drug that's a mysterious cure-all to some sickness that he knew I had before I even did."

"Exactly."

"Plus, he was super sketchy about that body we saw in the park." I had been saying this to myself in the shower every morning, trying to detach from the phrase and the event enough that I wouldn't shudder every time the words left my mouth, and I thought I just about pulled it off. "Didn't that strike you as weird? I was a mess after that date, and he didn't even seem like anything particularly alarming had happened. He didn't even want to call the cops, Cecile."

She frowned. "That was weird, yeah. Well, how are we going to stalk him? Do you even know where he lives?"

"I know what his car looks like."

"You just want to drive around town until we see his car? Rena, that's insane."

I bit my lip and mumbled, "It is, isn't it?"

"We'll use Google Earth." She reached behind her and pulled her laptop out of the backpack hanging on the back of her chair.

"What? How?"

"This town's not that big." She was already typing, focused intently on the screen. "And there can't be that many bright yellow cars. We'll map them all and just follow each one up until we find him."

* * *

There were seven bright yellow cars in town, it turned out. We ruled one of them out automatically because it was clearly a Hummer, and Cryder drove a sedan. Cecile created a map that would lead us from one car to the next and uploaded it to her phone. She also insisted that we each wear sunglasses and tuck our hair into hats.

"To stay undercover," she explained, helping me push my ponytail into her father's old Chicago Cubs baseball cap.

"You're having way too much fun."

"What's wrong with fun? Besides, you don't want him to recognize you, do you?'

"He knows what your car looks like, Cecile."

She shrugged. "Maybe he doesn't remember."

"Can we just get going?'

She tipped her sunglasses at me and pulled out of the driveway. "Sure thing, stalker."

"I'm not a stalker."

"This is excellent, you know. I never thought you'd want to do something like this."

I didn't answer her. The truth was, I didn't want to do this. I wanted a normal boyfriend, one who wouldn't make me feel the need to disguise myself and drive around town spying on him. One who wouldn't take me on dates where dead bodies showed up. With a boy like that, a normal one, Cecile would have been right—I never would have wanted to do this. Cryder was so weird that he was making me weird.

The first two cars on our map weren't Cryder's. The first one we passed was about a hundred years old, so egregiously rusted that I couldn't possibly mistake it with Cryder's semi-new, tidy vehicle. The second one was packed with baby toys and a car seat.

"Is this it?" Cecile asked, coasting slowly past a driveway so we could get a good look at the third possibility.

I peered out the window. It certainly looked like Cryder's car. "I think it might be."

"Do you remember the license plate?"

"No."

"We should really start memorizing the license plates of the guys we date."

"That's creepy, Cecile. Who does that?"

"I don't know. Who does any of this?"

"Touché."

She turned the car around and parked it on the side of the street about a block away. "Let's wait here a while and see what happens."

"You don't think we should knock on the door?"

"If he was going to answer any questions to your face, he'd have done it already. We need to get some dirt on him. Catch him doing something he can't explain away. Then we can confront him."

I didn't answer. I didn't want to see Cryder doing anything he couldn't explain away. I was still holding out hope for him to be a decent guy.

Cecile sunk down in her seat, and after a moment I did too. I looked out over the dashboard at the house. It was small but incredibly well-maintained. The other homes on the street ranged from cared for to totally unkempt, but the house that might've been Cryder's was one of the nicest. The white paint was fresh, and the lawn looked as if it had been mowed yesterday. Even the grass looked greener.

"Look," Cecile hissed.

The door was opening. I dropped lower in my seat, so low that all I could see of Cryder as he emerged was the top of his head. He locked the door, looked around as if he sensed our eyes on him, and then made his way to his car. He climbed in and backed out of the driveway.

"What do we do?' I asked.

In answer, Cecile started the engine and pulled slowly away from the curb.

"Don't get too close," I said.

"Obviously."

My only experience of Cryder's driving so far had been reckless and frightening, but to be fair that was in an emergency situation. So, I was relieved to see that he was more reserved now. He kept to the speed limit and stopped at every stop sign. Of course, his responsible driving probably meant that he was also doing regular mirror checks, which meant he was more likely to notice we were behind him… "Fall back a little," I told Cecile.

"Would you stop being so paranoid?'

"You're the one who made us put on costumes!" Fighting under our breath was increasing the air of secrecy around the whole thing. I felt like a covert operative in an intelligence agency, like the stakes were much higher than they really were. The truth was that if Cryder caught us, I'd look like an idiot and he probably wouldn't want to see me again, but we wouldn't be in any danger.

At least, I didn't think we would.

Of course, I hadn't thought we'd find a dead body on our first date, either.

Actually, who knew how serious this situation was? "Cecile, please," I said.

She let out a frustrated huff and tapped the brake, letting Cryder pull several more feet ahead. "If he makes two turns in a row, I'll lose him, Rena."

I rubbed my palms on my jeans. They were starting to sweat. "I just don't want us to get caught."

Cryder stopped outside the grocery store. He didn't park, though, just put on his flashers and left the car running at the curb right outside the doors. Cecile pulled into a parking space at the back of the lot, where we could keep his car in view. "What is he doing?"

"Shopping, I guess. This is pretty normal behavior." I let out a relieved breath.

Her eyes were narrowed. "Maybe."

"Maybe?"

"Why doesn't he just park, if he's shopping?"

"He probably just had to run in for one thing."

"That's kind of weird."

"Not as weird as the rest of it."

"Still."

"You're reaching, Cecile."

"I thought you wanted to know what he was up to."

"Yeah, well, I wanted it to be nothing."

"Let's wait and see."

A moment later Cryder emerged with a single grocery bag. "Wish we could see what he has in there," Cecile murmured, as he got back into his car and pulled away. We followed after him again.

Part of me wanted to snap at her, or maybe laugh at her, but there was part of me that agreed. What one thing had he gone to the store for? It seemed like there was a lot to learn from that little piece of information.

Oh, God. I was being obsessive.

I wished suddenly that I'd had more experience with guys, so I could at least reassure myself that it was definitely Cryder's vagueness and mystery that was making me act this way. That this wasn't something about me. I didn't want to be the kind of girl who stalked my boyfriends, looking for something to be wrong. I wanted to trust them.

I wanted to trust him.

"Maybe we should just go home," I told Cecile.

She turned onto an empty street. "Shit."

"Where'd he go?"

"I lost him." She pounded the steering wheel in frustration. "I knew we should've stayed on his tail."

"Turn left here."

"Why?"

"I don't know, I'm guessing." If we didn't find him, we'd go home, I promised myself.

Cecile swung the wheel—

BLAM! There was a sound like a gunshot, or an explosion. The car veered precariously. A scream erupted, too, and it took me a second to realize it was coming from me.

"Rena, calm down!" Cecile had both hands on the wheel. "It's a blowout. It's okay." A moment later the car was stopped, and her hands were on my arms. "Hey. It's fine. Just the tire. We're fine."

I forced my breathing to return to normal. "I hate cars." It came out in a gasp.

"I know." She squeezed my hands.

"Do you know how to change a tire?"

"I'll call AAA"

Three sharp raps came on the window. My gaze darted up. Cecile turned and rolled the window down just a crack.

"Need a hand, ladies?"

I sucked in a breath. It was the guy from the bookstore, the linebacker type I'd met right before meeting Cryder.

"I'm Bristol," he said, and smiled, showing all his teeth.

Chapter Eight

"WE"VE GOT THIS UNDER CONTROL," CECILE said. I could almost see her hackles go up. She hated unsolicited offers of help from men, never mind the fact that we actually didn't know how to change the tire and, if it weren't for her AAA membership, help would've been something we could really use right now. It was the kind of thing that would've annoyed me under ordinary circumstances—really, I'm a feminist too, but there's a time and a place—but Bristol creeped me out so much that I was glad she was dismissing him.

"You sure?' He stepped back a little, toward the tire and out of my view. "This is pretty bad. I think your rim might be bent."

"Shit. Really?' Cecile got out of the car. Immediately I felt uneasy. I didn't trust him alone with her. I scrambled out the passenger door and around to where they were standing, eyeing the blown tire critically.

"Look here," he said, tracing a finger along the side of the wheel. "See how it's a little caved in?'

"Not really…"

Bristol looked up at me, and for the first time I noticed how dark his eyes were. I almost couldn't make out the irises at all. I didn't remember this from our bookstore encounter. Hadn't his eyes looked more normal then? I wasn't sure. "How about you?" he asked. "You see it, right?"

I crouched down beside him to examine the wheel. "I'm not sure."

"AAA will handle it for us," Cecile said firmly.

"I could do it." Bristol's face stretched into a smile that seemed vaguely menacing. Was it just me? "Wouldn't charge you anything."

"No thank you."

"I'll wait with you, then," he suggested, rising smoothly to his feet. "Two young girls shouldn't be alone on the side of the road."

"We're fine, thanks."

"No, no. I really wouldn't feel right."

I started to stand up, to back Cecile up in her insistence that we were fine on our own—this wasn't exactly a bad neighborhood, and anyway, it was daytime, for God's sake— but before I could rise, a couple of dark spots on the cuffs of Bristol's pants caught my eye.

Red spots.

The same red I'd seen on my fingers on my date with Cryder.

Blood.

Oh, God. Could Bristol be the murderer? Suddenly my

thoughts were racing. I'd met him just before meeting Cryder—Cryder, who was acting incredibly strange about the entire incident, who had been nothing but vague and suspicious with me. What if they knew each other? What if Cryder was protecting Bristol, and that's why he'd been so hesitant to call the police? Or what if...what if they were in cahoots?

And here we were, stranded, alone with Bristol.

I edged close to Cecile. "Can we talk for a second?"

"What's up?"

"Um." I had to think fast, to come up with something that wouldn't make him suspect. "I need a tampon." That ought to put him off. Boys couldn't handle periods, everyone knew that.

"I think there's one in my purse," Cecile said.

"Great, would you mind?"

"You can get it."

Oh my God, could she be more difficult? "I don't want to go in your purse, Cecile." I met her gaze and widened my eyes, hoping she'd understand what I meant—that there was something I wasn't saying right now. If she pointed out that we went into each other's purses all the time, I'd be screwed.

The pause was excruciating. Then, "Okay. Come on, I'll see if I have something for you."

I followed her around the car, heart in my throat. Cecile opened the back door and we both leaned in. "What's up?" she hissed. "This isn't really about a tampon, is it?"

"No. It's Bristol. He has blood on his pants."

"What are you saying?"

"I think he might be the murderer, Cecile."

She stared. "You're jumping to conclusions."

"I met him once before and he was super shady then. He doesn't go to our school even though he's the right age. Now he shows up and wants to hang out with us while we're stranded? This feels really dangerous, Cecile. I think we need to get out of here."

"I can't leave the car!"

"AAA's coming. Lock it and we'll run. Into the woods, okay? When we're safe we'll call AAA and explain what happened."

"Fuck." She exhaled hard. "He is creepy."

"We need to move now before he catches on."

"Okay. Okay."

We backed slowly out of the car. I put my hand on the open passenger door and mimed slamming it, then pointed to the woods behind us.

Cecile nodded.

I held up one finger. She palmed her key fob, her thumb over the lock button.

I held up my second finger.

We both breathed in.

SLAM!

The door locks beeped as Cecile pressed down on the key fob, but I was already in a dead sprint. I heard her behind me, gasping, her footfalls heavy against the packed earth. I couldn't tell if Bristol was following us or not, but I didn't dare look back. Main Street was on the other side of these woods, about a quarter mile from where we'd left the car. If we reached it, we'd be surrounded by people. We'd be safe.

Run, Rena. Keep going.

I wasn't an athlete. I'd never been able to run long distances, and when we did the mile run in gym class I usually finished near the end. Cecile would have been surpassing me easily right about now, except she was wearing heels. I wondered if she'd had the sense to kick them off when we left the car. Running barefoot through the woods certainly wasn't ideal either, though. Her feet could be getting all cut up. Again, I was tempted to look behind me, to make sure my friend was keeping up. But I didn't dare.

Then I heard a roar of outrage. The voice was deep and powerful and definitely didn't belong to Cecile. Bristol. So, he was chasing us. Which meant...which meant he had to be the murderer. If he was truly just a friendly passerby trying to help us with a flat tire, he'd be baffled by our flight. He wouldn't be in pursuit. I felt a fleeting sense of vindication—we were right to run—followed by abject terror. A murderer was chasing us through the woods. I bore down and tried to run faster, but my breath burned in my lungs and my torso felt like one giant cramp. I was going to give out soon.

We're not going to make it.

Cecile's breathing had taken on a sort of whimper, and I wondered if she was starting to wear out too or if she'd hurt herself. If she fell, there was no way I'd be able to carry her and keep up anything resembling my current pace. We must be almost to town, right? I thought desperately. But the truth was, I had no clear idea of how far we'd come or how far we had yet to go. Worse yet, I didn't know how close Bristol was. For all I knew his hand could grab my shoulder, pulling me back toward him, at any moment. Never in my life, not even when I'd woken up alone in the hospital after my parents' car crash, could I remember feeling such abject terror.

I had to know. I risked a glance over my shoulder. There was Cecile, right on my heels, her face contorted almost unrecognizably by fear and exertion. I didn't see Bristol, which gave me a moment of relief, but then he roared again. It sounded closer than before.

A fresh thrill of fear shot through me. He's gaining on us.

Suddenly my body pitched forward. I jerked my head back around as the ground rushed up to meet me. I tried to take the impact on my hands, but my forward momentum propelled me over and into a roll. I came up on my knees, vaguely aware that my palms were skinned and full of dirt. In some far corner of my mind that wasn't swamped with fear, I was surprised it didn't hurt more…

Then I saw what I'd tripped over.

A girl lay on the ground, limbs sprawled awkwardly around her, hair tangled and dirty. She was about my own age, probably, and so pale that she was almost translucent. A split second later I saw the blood, cold and tacky, on her neck and shoulder. Her eyes were slightly open. She didn't move.

She was dead.

"Oh my God." Cecile's voice came from behind me,

wavering all over the place. "Is that Caitlin Bessier?"

I looked again. Caitlin was a year behind us in school, and I didn't know her well. She was a lively, bouncy, flirtatious girl, always immaculately dressed and wearing a dazzling smile. It was hard to square that image with this pale, lifeless girl. Still… "I think that's her skirt. I think I've seen her wearing that."

"Shit," Cecile breathed.

I got my feet under me. "We have to go. We have to go now."

Cecile squatted down. "Rena, look at this."

"Cecile!"

"Look."

It was her I'm-not-taking-no-for-an-answer tone, and I knew it would be fastest not to argue. I bent down. Cecile had lifted a clump of Caitlin's hair away from her neck. "What is that?"

I stared. Two small wounds, each about the size of my smallest fingernail, sat side by side on her neck. "Snakebite?"

"What the hell kind of snake…."

There was a crashing in the brush behind us. Bristol. "Can we talk about this later?"

"Yeah." Cecile jumped to her feet—she was barefoot, I noticed—and set off running again. I ran after her. Maybe it was because of the break, or maybe I was just in shock, but my muscles and lungs weren't complaining as loudly as they had been. All I could think about was the dead girl in the woods, the second body I'd encountered in a matter of weeks. What was going on in this town? And why did it seem to be following me around?

Getting to town ahead of Bristol suddenly took on new importance. This was about more than just keeping me—and Cecile—safe from whatever he intended for us. The police station was on Main Street. If we kept ahead of him, we could go straight there and tell them everything we knew. We could tell them about Bristol's sudden appearances in suspicious circumstances, the blood on his pants, and how he'd chased us through the woods, and surely that would be enough to render him a suspect. We could prevent anyone else from dying.

God, Caitlin. She was only a sophomore. All my memories of her were tinged with mild annoyance—she was too loud, too perky, and too giggly. She was like Cecile, but without brains or wit. But of course, I'd barely known her. Had we ever even had one conversation? I'd judged her and completely written her off without ever giving her a chance, and now she was gone.

Cecile overtook me with a cry of, "Come on, Rena!" I focused on her pounding footfalls and forced myself to run harder. I could hear a lot of rustling now, the crunch of leaves and branches being shoved out of the way, and the thump overlapping thump of feet hitting the earth. How close were we? How close was he?

"There's...steeple!" Cecile gasped out, pointing ahead. Through a gap in the trees, I could make out the tall white peak of the Main Street Chapel. We were almost there...

Something struck my back with incredible force,

driving the air out of my lungs and propelling me forward so fast I didn't have time to get my hands under me. I landed face down in the dirt, sending a bolt of pain through my body. When I tried to scramble to my feet, I couldn't. A strong arm held me down.

"Gotcha," Bristol's voice grated out, deep and laced with a sinister delight.

Chapter Nine

HIS BREATH WAS HOT ON MY NECK AND his fingers dug into my shoulders so hard I was worried they might be about to draw blood. "We met too early," he said, his voice almost a hiss. "You weren't ready for me then, were you? But you are now, you're nearly ripe…"

Cecile screamed, her voice seeming to come from very far away, and I heard the wet crunch of a body taking a blow. Bristol's weight shifted on my back, but not enough to let me up.

"Cecile, go get help!" I half-cried, half-gasped. "Cecile," Bristol said, "If you move an inch, I'll kill her so fast you won't even see it happen."

Fear spiraled out from my heart to each of my limbs. I flexed with it. It should have given me power –adrenaline– but Bristol's strength was too much for me to hope to overpower him. Somewhere behind me, Cecile was breathing in short, whimpering gasps and I knew she'd been too afraid to run for help. He's going to kill me anyway, I thought. He's going to kill me, and because she's not a threat, he's going to take his time. And then he's going to kill her.

I thought about the puncture wounds we'd seen on Caitlin's neck when we'd passed her body in the forest. What made that kind of mark? What was Bristol about to do to me?

And what had he meant when he said I was nearly ripe?

As if in answer to my silent question, he stroked two fingers along the side of my neck and began to speak. "You're a danger, you know, Rena," he said. "Such a little girl, but you're a threat. Did you know that? Do you know how many of us live in fear of you?"

I couldn't make sense of his words. I wasn't sure I wanted to. Maybe he was insane.

He shifted his weight again. "Stand up."

I was terrified to obey him. I didn't want to give him anything he wanted. But the temptation of being free of his gruesome hold was too much to refuse. I scrambled to my feet.

"Don't run," he said softly. "You know I can catch you."

I backed away. I couldn't help it. I put five feet between us, then ten…

And in a heartbeat, Bristol had closed the gap. I didn't even see him move. One moment he was leaning against a tree and watching me edge away from him, the next, he had me by the throat. "I told you not to run from me, Rena. Don't overestimate your own power. The others might live in fear of you, but I don't. I know you're no danger as long as you have no idea what you are."

I tried to speak but couldn't. His grip on my throat was

too tight.

"She can't breathe!" Cecile's voice was a shriek.

"She's changing," he practically crooned, stroking my cheek with the back of his hand. "She's different, isn't she? Yes, almost finished, almost done. But not quite, are you, little girl? Enough of what you were still remains. And until you've finished your metamorphosis, you'll never be able to overpower me. Even Cryder knows that."

"How do you know Cryder?' Cecile asked.

I didn't want to know the answer. I could only think of one possibility. Cryder must be his partner in crime, his accomplice in committing the gristly murders we'd encountered. That was the only explanation that answered everything, from the reason Cryder hadn't wanted to involve the police to Cryder's mysterious drink. It wasn't a vitamin drink at all. They were giving me something to weaken me, to make me less of a threat, so that they'd be able to kill me. It must have been the plan all along.

Except...except why would I have ever been considered a threat? Bristol easily had a hundred pounds on me. He'd relaxed his grip some, enough that I could breathe comfortably, but he was restraining me with no effort, and I was sure he could crush my windpipe if he wanted to. He claimed he wasn't afraid of me, but the question remained— why was anybody? How did they know who she was? There were so many more questions, that she didn't have the time to ask or even find an answer for at that moment.

Bristol's voice jerked my attention back to him. "Cryder

and I have more in common than you can imagine."

"No. Cryder's nothing like you." I could hear the lack of conviction in Cecile's voice.

Bristol must have heard it too, because he laughed. "You're not really sure what Cryder's like, are you?"

"He was kind to us…"

"He appeared in your lives out of nowhere. Just like I did. He frightened you and confused you, didn't he? Admit it."

"There's nothing unusual about being wary of a stranger. That doesn't mean anything."

I closed my eyes. Cecile, stop fighting. Why was she so determined to stick up for Cryder?

"Didn't you wonder why he chose Rena so quickly?" Bristol turned back to me. "Didn't you question why he wanted you? You didn't think he saw you—you—on the street and fell in love, did you? You're a foolish girl, but you can't be that naive."

I had wondered. Of course, I had. I'd never let myself articulate the idea, but Bristol was right. Cryder had fallen for me much too quickly. What did he even know about me?

"All right," Cecile said, and her voice had taken on the wry overtones she used when she was about to score a point in an argument. I usually hated that voice, because it meant I was about to be shown up, but right now all I heard was confidence. Maybe her confidence was misplaced, but it gave me hope. "Tell us, then. What was Cryder doing with Rena?"

Bristol laughed, a short burst. "Were you jealous?"

A pause. "I don't see the relevance."

"You were. You couldn't understand why anyone would choose her over you."

"Is that true?" I asked. Cecile was charming, and she'd always had a way with guys. She'd never pined after a guy, at least as far as I was aware—they threw themselves at her and she blew through them, never allowing herself to get tied down. I, meanwhile, had never had a boyfriend or even been kissed. Until Cryder, that is. Could she really be jealous now that I was finally getting some attention?

"Don't listen to this crap, Rena," Cecile said.

"That's right, Rena," Bristol agreed. "She doesn't understand you, does she? She has no idea how special you are. She's never known." His voice dropped a degree in pitch and volume. "You'd like to make her pay, wouldn't you?"

Yes. The thought bubbled up from somewhere deep and primal within me, somewhere I didn't know existed. I was appalled the moment it entered my mind, yet I couldn't pretend it hadn't existed. I couldn't deny that warm, bitter satisfaction I'd felt at the idea of...of hurting Cecile, making her see that I wasn't just some loser to be brushed aside. I deserved to be noticed.

No. What was wrong with me? I flinched away from myself in horror. Of course, I didn't want to hurt Cecile. It wasn't her fault guys liked her, for God's sake. And if she'd ever felt a moment of jealousy about my date—relationship?— with Cryder, she hadn't let me see it.

"Cryder saw the truth about you," Bristol murmured. "Cryder saw the danger. I see it too."

"What danger?" Cecile demanded.

"You're stalling." His eyes cut sideways at her. "I know. I see what you're doing. You're trying to distract me. You're hoping someone will find us. He released my neck and I fell to my knees. I needed to run. I needed to get my feet under me and run, go to town, get help. Put as much distance as possible between myself and this...this beast of a man. But he was stalking Cecile now, edging closer to her. She backed away from him until she was pressed against the trunk of a tree, and he leaned in, his handsome, terrible face inches from hers.

"No one's going to find us, Cecile," he said.

I felt like screaming.

"Prevailing wisdom is that you shouldn't play with your food, isn't it?" He leaned close to her, obscenely, intimately close. Like a lover. "But it's just so tempting."

"What are you talking about?" I breathed.

"Oh, Rena." Bristol shook his head, not turning his gaze from Cecile. "You're the last to know, aren't you? Always the last to know. Even your friend is starting to wonder, aren't you, Cecile? Even she has a guess. But you...you'd never have figured it out."

"Figured what out?" The words were out before I could decide whether I truly wanted the answer.

Bristol's answering chuckle was low and horrible. "What we are."

Again, he moved so quickly that I couldn't track him. One moment he was leering at Cecile, the next, he had me backed up against a tree trunk, the rough bark scraping my shoulders. His face was contorted into a horrible snarl. As I watched, something seemed to shift in his mouth, and another set of teeth lowered over his incisors.

No, not teeth.

Fangs.

He caught my eyes with his, and with a rush of horror, I noticed that the color of his eyes was changing, brightening. Burgundy. Maroon. Red. Bright, blood red.

What we are, he'd said. What.

Not a murderer.

Not even human.

He bent close and sniffed the artery in my neck, hummed with pleasure, and I thought, vampire, vampire, but how could it be?

"Rena!" Cecile's voice was pure panic now, no more stalling, no more games. Her head appeared over Bristol's shoulder—she'd jumped onto his back—but he threw her off easily. Her body hit the ground with a thump and I gasped, but Bristol's hand was already around my throat. This time, he held tight. I gagged and my eyes watered, and I tried to bat him off, but he was strong. So strong. Inhumanly strong.

This is really happening. He's a vampire.

I thought of the bloody corpse under the bench in the park, and of poor Caitlin lying on the forest floor, and as Bristol's lips met my neck I knew, beyond any doubt, that my fate would be the same as theirs. I prayed silently that Cecile would escape, that she hadn't been hurt too badly when he'd thrown her. Maybe she had already run away. Maybe she wouldn't have to watch this.

God, don't let her have to watch this.

God, don't let me be alone when I die.

I felt the pressure of bone, of Bristol's (vampire) fangs at my neck, and my final thought was of Cryder and the fact that I would never learn whether he'd meant to harm me, or if, by chance, whatever we'd had was real.

Chapter Ten

MY VISION ENDED...DARKENED...BLACKENED...
And then returned.

I gasped, my lungs grasping almost involuntarily at air, hauling oxygen back into my bloodstream. My throat burned, but with every breath, my vision cleared, and I became more aware of my senses. My hearing returned. The tight grip of Bristol's hand around my throat. It had loosened, though...why?

He wasn't looking at me.

He was looking off to the left. I followed his gaze. Cecile.

She lay where Bristol had thrown her, unmoving, eyes closed. I couldn't tell if she was breathing or not. Blood gushed from somewhere beneath a clump of hair. That could mean anything, though, I reminded myself. Head wounds like to bleed. We'd learned that in health class, during our first aid unit. Head wounds often look scarier than they really are. She might be okay. She might just have a concussion, or...

Bristol sniffed the air.

It was inhuman, that sniff. His ears nearly perked up. He looked like a dog—like a wolf—scenting prey.

Vampire.

Scenting blood.

With the same superhuman speed he'd already demonstrated, he released me and moved to her. Crouching over her prone body, he lowered his nose to the blood pooling around her head and inhaled deeply. When he lifted his head, his eyes were closed and the expression on his face was one of rapture.

I was going to be sick.

Summoning every ounce of energy in my oxygen-deprived muscles, I launched myself at Bristol. I should have run, probably—hadn't I just been hoping that Cecile would take advantage of Bristol's distraction with me to make her own escape?—but I couldn't. It was too much to ask. In the end, I doubted Cecile could have done it either. We'd been friends for too long. We were too deeply bonded. The idea of running away while this...this thing crouched over her sniffing at her blood was almost as repulsive as Bristol himself. If I'd abandoned her, I too would've been an animal.

Vampire.

He's going to kill me, I thought, just before my body made impact with Bristol's. Surely the idea of my own imminent demise should have lost some of its power by now? If only I'd known I was going to die, known it for sure, this would've all been much easier. Instead I kept finding false hope, believing I had a chance at escape. Without my even realizing it, when Bristol had released me, I'd found hope again. But no. I was truly at the end of the line.

I drove into him hard, like an egg against a brick wall. I was surprised not to be liquefied. I'd never thought of the human body as pliant before, but Bristol's muscles made him rock hard. The impact bruised me. Still, I couldn't give up. My only chance was to distract him from Cecile, to turn his attention back to me. Maybe if I could do that long enough to persuade him to kill me first, she'd be able to recover consciousness and run away. Or maybe...maybe someone would find us...

No. Stop hoping, Rena. You're on your own.

I beat my fists against Bristol's back, and he let out a fearsome roar.

As he got to his feet, I wrapped my legs around his waist. I wouldn't let him throw me off the way he had thrown Cecile. Hanging on tight with my thigh muscles, I continued my assault on his upper body, searching for weak spots. I found none. I slammed my fist into his neck, prompting a howl, but it seemed fueled more by rage than pain. I tried slamming the heel of my hand into his nose, but the angle was awkward, and I missed and connected with his cheekbone. That blow probably did more damage to me than to him.

"Cecile!" I screamed.

She didn't stir.

"Cecile, please!"

Bristol whipped his body, shaking me from side to side,

determined to throw me. I clung to him more fiercely, breathing hard, equally determined to maintain my hold. My ankles found each other, and I locked them together, tightening my grip on his broad torso. I wrapped one arm around his neck, bringing my forearm to bear like a rod against his throat, and pulled it tight by wrapping my other arm around that wrist. I'd learned the technique from Cecile, who had learned it from her father, an army veteran. The idea was to cut off your adversary's air supply, which seemed fitting—I would do to Bristol what he had done to me.

He huffed out something that sounded like a laugh. "Can't choke me, Rena."

His voice was raspy, devoid of air. He was lying. I pulled tighter.

"Don't need to breathe," he hissed. "You can make me...quiet...can't make me die. Not this way."

I felt cold, then hot. "You're lying–."

"No reason."

"–to make me let you go."

He choked out another laugh. "Don't care. Don't let go. Doesn't matter."

Suddenly we were moving in a direction I didn't understand. Were we flying? Could vampires fly, on top of everything?

No. My back struck the ground with such force that the shock of it very nearly made me let go of Bristol. He had turned a somersault in midair and come down on his back. On my back. I was lucky not to have been seriously injured.

You're going to die anyway, I reminded myself. Distract him. Take up his time.

"Stubborn," Bristol grunted. "Parasite."

"You're the one who feeds on people."

He got to his feet and I braced myself for another flip, another impact on my back, but this time we moved in a different direction. When the impact came, it wasn't as hard as the last strike had been, but sharp spikes of pain bit into the flesh of my back. I cried out. He was pushing me into the bark of a tree.

"Let go," he hissed. "Let go and this ends."

"You won't let me live."

He rubbed his back—my back—up and down the bark, and it scraped and gouged at me. I could only imagine the dirt that was being pushed into the wounds he was digging in my skin, and I bit back a sob of pain.

"I'll let you die," he said.

And, God. I wanted to say yes.

It was going to happen anyway. Just let it be now. Just let it end.

Cecile…

But she wasn't waking up. I couldn't save her.

I released Bristol's body and slipped to the ground behind him. A hair's breadth of a second later, he was facing me again, his hand back at my throat, and this time, the pressure didn't stop. It lifted.

He was holding me up by my neck.

I closed my eyes.

"Rena!" someone shouted. A new voice. Not Cecile.

My eyes snapped open. Cryder?

He was standing several yards behind Bristol, his eyes wide with fear and rage and something I couldn't quite identify. A light seemed to shine from them as his gaze caught and held mine. Our eye contact couldn't have lasted more than a second, but it felt as if everything, from the moment we'd gotten the flat tire to our desperate flight through the woods to the blood I knew was rising through the back of my sweater, had been leading to this moment. Looking at Cryder now, it seemed unfathomable that I had ever questioned him. It didn't matter what Bristol said, that he had suggested he and Cryder had been together the whole time. One look was enough to tell me the truth. Cryder's arrival meant my safety.

Bristol hadn't even turned to look. "You're too late," he said softly.

"No–." I choked.

"She's mine. And the other one, she's dead."

"No!" The word ripped itself from my lungs. "Cecile!"

Bristol bared his fangs at me...

Cryder lunged. He barreled toward both of us so fast that I couldn't hold back a scream, but somehow, he managed to strike only Bristol, peeling him away from his stance in front of me. I backed around to the far side of the tree I'd been pressed up against and peeked out to watch, panting to catch my breath. They fought vigorously, terrifyingly, too quickly to track their motions. I couldn't tell who was winning. Watching them now, I realized fully how much danger I'd been in. Bristol could have snapped my bones in one hand. Cryder...Cryder could have broken my neck if he'd been careless while we were kissing. How could I have allowed him to touch me?

Even now, watching him, I wanted to do it again.

He could lift me, I thought. He could hurt me. But he didn't.

The brawl rolled to the right a little, and Cecile came into view. Instinctively, I ran for her. I dropped to my knees beside her and grabbed her hand. "Cecile? Oh, God, please wake up. We need to get out of here. Cecile."

She remained motionless. I tried to remember CPR. Did you even give someone CPR for a head wound? No, it was for a stopped heart, wasn't it? I should check her pulse. I fumbled with her wrist, trying to find the telltale beats that would let me know she was all right, but I found nothing.

She's dead, Bristol had said. Was he right?

"She isn't dead," came a voice, as if it was reading my mind.

Startled, I looked up. A man I didn't recognize stood over us. He was older than me, older than Cryder or Bristol, but not by much. In his twenties, maybe. "Who are you?"

He didn't look at me. Instead, he sank to his knees and took Cecile's wrist from my hand. "You're looking in the wrong place," he said. "You can feel the pulse here..." he moved his fingers to her neck, just under her jawbone, "or here."

"She's alive?"

"Yes. But fading."

"Who are you?'

"Forgive me. My name is Drake."

"Drake like the hip-hop artist?'

"If you like."

"You're with them." I gestured to Bristol and Cryder.

It was an accusation, and Drake knew it. "I'm with...Cryder. Yes."

"You're like them."

"Yes."

"What are you?'

For the first time, he met my eyes. "I think you know the answer to that, Rena."

"How do you know my name?'

"The same way Bristol knew to hunt you. The same way Cryder knew you needed his concoction—" he sniffed. "You've been drinking it, good girl."

"How do you know that?'

"Rena, please. There will be time for answers, I promise. But right now, you must decide: do you want your friend to live?'

"What?'

"I can save her," he said. "I can save her right here and now. But there's only one way. She's too far gone to be taken to a hospital. Too much blood has been lost."

"What are you going to do? Are you a doctor?'

"Rena."

"Of course, I want you to save her! What kind of

question is that?" I was breathing too fast, near tears. I was angry and panicked and felt like screaming. Cecile lay dying—nearly gone—on the ground in front of me, and we were talking about whether I wanted her saved? Why were we talking at all? "Save her!"

"Rena, you have to understand. You have to calm down. You're her best friend, yes? Like family?"

"Yes. Yes. We're...we're sisters. Oh, God, Cecile..."

"You can make this decision for her."

"She's here because of me. I'm the one who wanted us to follow Cryder. I'm the one Bristol wanted. If it weren't for me."

"Be quiet." Drake's voice was sharp. "Listen to me, Rena. In minutes it will be too late. I can save her, but in order to do it, you'll have to give her up. The friend, the...the sister you know will be preserved, but she will lose herself in the process. Do you understand?"

"No," I whispered, suddenly terrified beyond anything I'd felt so far.

"If I save her," Drake said, holding my gaze, "she'll be like me."

"Like you?" Vampire.

"Like me and Cryder." And Bristol, he didn't say, but I saw his eyes cut towards the fight before returning to me.

They were gold, his eyes, and shining.

Like Cryder's. Not like Bristol's.

I swallowed the bile that was rising in my throat and squeezed my best friend's hand. "Do it."

Chapter Eleven

DRAKE'S EYES DARKENED. AT FIRST, I THOUGHT it was a trick of the light, but before long the shining golden color had faded to a matte yellow-brown, and then to black. With everything I saw from these people, every weird little behavior, I was more and more frightened. Every moment I spent with them, they seemed less and less human.

Drake bared his teeth, showing fangs where the canine teeth should be, longer than normal teeth and tapered to a point. There was something odd about that—odder than the existence of fangs in the mouth of this guy in front of me—and it took me a while to put my finger on it. It wasn't until he raised his own wrist to his lips and bit down that I realized—he wasn't menacing. He didn't have a snarl on his face, and he didn't look as if he was trying to show me his fangs to scare me. He'd simply opened his mouth and there they were.

He can't help it, I thought.

What difference does that make? He's still a vampire!

But he's saving Cecile…

I didn't know. I couldn't tell who the good guys were

anymore, who I should trust and who I should fear. I just watched, dazed, as Drake held his arm back out. He was bleeding now, from two puncture wounds that seemed deep. I knew they'd match the fangs I'd seen. What was he going to do?

He tipped Cecile's head back and, using a thumb, held her chin to open her mouth. The other arm, the bleeding one, he lifted over her face, angling it so that drops of blood fell on her tongue. It took me a moment to register what he was doing. By the time I did, he'd finished and was holding her body in an upright position in his arms. She looked like she'd fallen asleep sitting up.

He'd fed her blood. I gagged but swallowed hard against it. He was doing what I'd told him to do, I reminded myself, although that didn't make me feel much better. And I trusted Drake. I honestly believed he was here for Cecile's benefit, that he'd meant what he said about wanting to save her. Something was at work here that I didn't understand, that was for sure, and it would be a mistake for me to try to involve myself in it.

Suddenly, a loud growl came from behind me, accompanied by something that was closer to a whimper. Drake's head jerked up in alarm. I spun around. In my horror over what was happening to Cecile, I'd managed to forget all about Bristol and Cryder fighting behind me. Now I saw that they'd separated a little and were circling each other, like boxers preparing for the next blow. Cryder had a hand pressed to his shoulder, his face contorted in a grimace. As I watched, Bristol spat a mouthful of blood and flesh onto the ground and smiled, his face masked with blood.

I retched.

Drake grabbed my arm and pulled me back. His eyes met mine. "You should run," he said.

"I'm not leaving Cecile."

He nodded. "I thought you would say that."

I was prepared to fight him more, but to my surprise, he conceded the point. Maybe he really did understand. He pulled me in closer to him and I got the feeling he was trying to shield me. Why? Bristol and Cryder were preoccupied with each other. They weren't paying any attention to me. If Cecile were awake, I'd have been willing to bet the two of us could get up and walk away from this nightmare, and neither of them would have even noticed we were gone.

Right?

Right?

It didn't feel right. Suddenly I felt cold. If this had nothing to do with me and I could truly just walk away from it, why had Cryder and Bristol both been so fascinated with me from the moment they'd laid eyes on me? I'd wanted to believe Cryder just had a crush, but if I was honest with myself, I'd known for a long time something more was at work here. The way I'd started to get sick and he'd immediately known what to do for me...that was no coincidence. And then there was the fact that, after cornering us in the woods, Bristol had focused his attention on me. He'd made it seem as though killing me was his top priority, and whatever happened to Cecile was just collateral damage.

For that matter, how had Cryder and Drake known where to find me?

Shrinking behind Drake now, I watched the exchange of blows between Cryder and Bristol, the horrible discoloration of Bristol's jaw from having bitten Cryder. As I looked on, Bristol landed a punch in Cryder's ribs. Cryder howled and crumpled to the ground. Bristol laughed.

"They're fighting about me," I said. "Aren't they?"

"It isn't quite that simple," Drake said.

"It's not complicated. Bristol wants to kill me. Cryder wants to stop him. Right?"

"Well, but…"

"That's right, isn't it?"

Drake didn't answer, but I didn't really need him to. I was capable of seeing what was happening right in front of me. This fight was because of me, and if Cryder were to come to harm, that would be because of me, too.

I darted out from behind Drake before he could stop me, knowing he would intervene if I gave him the chance, and ran to Cryder. "Bristol! Stop!"

To my surprise, he actually did stop, stepping back to regard me as I placed my body in front of Cryder's. His eyebrows disappeared into his shaggy hairline and he laughed. "You haven't had enough? I thought you'd know when to quit, girl."

"Rena!" Drake yelled.

I ignored him. "This isn't about Cryder. Let him go."

"I'm not keeping him, am I?" Bristol spread his arms.

"Cryder, you're free to go."

"You know I won't," Cryder spits. "Rena, get back."

"No."

"Get back." He got to his feet and staggered, obviously in pain.

"Cryder, you're bleeding, just...just stop. Please."

"My God," Bristol said softly, a bloody smile blooming on his lips. "You love him, don't you? You really love him."

My cheeks flamed. It's none of his business. I wanted desperately to be alone somewhere, just me and Cryder, to figure out what my feelings were, if I even had them. It felt so unfair that I had to do this here that my heart was searching for answers in the middle of a life or death scenario. I remembered watching Titanic when I was younger and thinking how romantic it all seemed, and how I couldn't wait to meet my own Leonardo DiCaprio. Only now did I realize how awful and ugly it was to realize you were in love with someone you might be just moments away from losing.

I turned my back to Cryder and faced Bristol. "I know what this is about."

"Do you?"

"It's about me. It's always been about me. I don't know why, but for some reason you want to kill me." I swallowed hard, trying not to let myself think about what I was doing. All that mattered was Cryder's ragged, pained breathing behind me. All that mattered was keeping Bristol from hurting him any more to get to me. "If you want me, just take me. I'll go with you."

"Rena, no." Cryder's voice was a sob.

I couldn't turn to him. If I saw his face, I might change my mind. "Cryder, you and Drake take Cecile. Save yourselves. Please. We don't all need to die here."

"No one needs to die here."

I wished I could believe that, but I just wasn't confident in Cryder's ability to win this fight. "It's all right, Cryder. I know what I'm doing."

"That's right, Cryder." Bristol smirked. "She knows what she's doing."

"Be safe," I said, and stepped toward Bristol.

Before I could register that he had moved, his hand was around my throat. The fact that I'd expected the attack didn't make it any less painful, and my body tried to gasp reflexively, but I couldn't draw breath. He peeled his upper lip back from his fangs, exposing them menacingly—so different from the way Drake had bared his before biting his wrist for Cecile. If I hadn't known better, I might have guessed the two were entirely different creatures.

Bristol lifted me into the air with one hand. My feet dangled, but I refused to kick at him. I wouldn't go out fighting. I wouldn't give my friends reason to question leaving me here. I closed my eyes and thought, I'm fine, I'm fine, I'm fine. This would all be over soon.

"You stupid, stupid girl," Bristol hissed. "This was never about killing you."

My eyes flew open.

"Killing you?" He scoffed. "As if I care whether you live

or die. All I care for is your blood."

My blood?

He sniffed at my neck again. A shiver ran through my skin like spiders were crawling over it. "So much power. When I've drained you, it'll all be mine. And then who will be able to stand in my way? Not your friends. They can start running now if they want, but once I'm done with you…" He licked behind my ear, and I recoiled internally disgusted. "I'll be nuclear. I'll be unstoppable. All thanks to you, you delicious bomb of a human. You'll give me the power I've always dreamed of."

Oh, God. I'd made a horrible mistake.

"Rena!" Cryder's voice was anguished.

Now I kicked out at Bristol, as hard as I could, but he dodged me easily and laughed. "Too late, girl. You should have run when you had the chance. You should have trusted Cryder more when he tried to save you. Now you'll both die in the end. So, will you, Drake, and—" He sniffed the air. "I see what you've done to that girl. She's not safe either, then. I hope you're all proud of yourselves."

I wanted to scream. All I'd wanted—so desperately— was to save Cryder. Instead, my rash actions were going to get everyone I loved killed. The one upside was that I wouldn't live to see it.

Bristol's hand squeezed my neck even tighter. The darkness started closing in, as the lack of air in my lungs made my vision dim. I closed my eyes and waited for it to be over.

But it never came.

Instead, I heard a tearing sound, accompanied by a

meaty squish—oh God, was this my death?—but suddenly breath rushed back into my lungs and I dropped to my hands and knees. My first inhale left my body in a soft scream, and I scrambled, trying to run away, but firm arms encircled me and held me. Tightly, not painfully. "Rena."

I opened my eyes.

Cryder.

He held me against his chest, his nose touching mine, his blue eyes inches from me. "Rena."

Exhausted, I let myself go limp in his arms.

Chapter Twelve

THE CLEARING WAS SUDDENLY, overwhelmingly, very quiet. I lay in Cryder's arms, listening to the incongruous sounds of birds singing around me. If it weren't for his hands on me and his heavy, strained breathing, I might have even thought I'd imagined the whole thing. Had we really been fighting for our lives? Surely it was just a misunderstanding. These things simply didn't happen in real life.   People didn't have fangs in real life.

But so much of my life over the past few weeks had been surreal. My mysteriously declining health, Cryder's curative elixir, and the fact that these new people had appeared as if from nowhere, seeming to know me. It was strange enough for a guy to show interest in me at all.

I couldn't deconstruct it right now. I focused on breathing, on keeping myself together.

"Rena," Cryder said. His voice was thick, as if he had been crying. "Are you hurt?"

I took stock of my body. My neck hurt quite a bit from

being squeezed repeatedly by Bristol, but other than that, I was all right. "I'm fine," I said, a tremble to my words.

He seemed to hear what I didn't say and trailed his fingers along my throat. "I'm so sorry about all this."

My body shook, from fear and possibly from the touch. "It isn't your fault," I told him. Then I reconsidered. "Is it?"

"It might be my fault."

I thought about that. Could Cryder be responsible for everything I had been through? No, I decided. Cryder was kind. He had genuinely wanted to help me at every turn, I was sure of that now. Even if he had led Bristol to me in some way, it wouldn't have been deliberate. I closed my eyes and felt his fingers on my neck, where Bristol had just handled me so roughly, and I knew the truth. Cryder would never hurt me.

"It isn't your fault," I told him.

"You shouldn't have done it," he said.

"Done what?"

"Charged in like that. You could have been killed."

I glared at him as I spoke. "You could have been killed."

He shook his head. "He didn't want to kill me. He only attacked me to get to you in the first place, Rena. It was very stupid on your part, diving in, trying to be a martyr without knowing the first thing about who Bristol is—who we are— and what he wanted with you. You see that now, don't you?"

"He wanted my blood…"

"Your blood." Cryder ran his thumb along my neck again, over the pulse point, and I was reminded of when Bristol had done the same thing. This is where he would have bitten me. This is where he wanted to drink from me.

"Why did he want my blood?" I asked, the question difficult to ask.

"It would have given him...great power," Cryder said. "Your blood is powerful, Rena. Transformative. If he had gotten it, he would have caught and killed me very quickly."

My own hand went to my neck. I felt hot, suddenly, lit up from inside, as if I could actually feel my powerful blood rushing through my veins? "Why?" I asked again. "What makes my blood so special?"

Cryder shook his head. "Another time. For now, let it be enough that Bristol is dead. He's no threat to you anymore."

So that was the awful deathlike sound I'd heard. I couldn't say I was surprised, but there was a part of me that wanted to cringe away from Cryder. A part of me that was horrified to be lying in the arms of a man who had so recently killed. Even if the victim was someone as evil—as inhuman—as Bristol, it came as a shock to realize that Cryder had it in him to commit such an act. Physically, I could never have overpowered Bristol, but even if I could have, I didn't think I'd have managed to take his life. It would've been too horrifying.

But he was going to kill Cecile...

Maybe. Maybe I could have done it for Cecile's sake.

I gazed up at Cryder. "You're hurt."

"I'm all right."

"No, you're bleeding."

"I'm healing."

I raised a hand to the wound on his arm. To my shock,

it did seem a little better than it had been before. "You're healing pretty fast," I managed.

He met my eyes. "We have a lot to talk about, Rena."

"You're like him, aren't you?"

"In some ways, yes. In many ways, no."

"I mean you're...what he is."

His face changed. Now he seemed to be pleading with me. "Rena..."

"Later, right?"

"I promise. But we shouldn't stay here."

On that, at least, I was in full agreement. Bristol might have been dead, but the clearing smelled like blood and it was making me want to vomit. Besides, we were sitting here at the scene of the crime. All it would take was for some innocent hiker to happen by, and we'd be looking at a lot more trouble than I wanted to deal with.

Oh, God. Was I really contemplating fleeing a crime scene? What had happened to me?

I didn't want to see it, but I forced myself to sit up, to extricate myself from Cryder's embrace and peek over his shoulder. There was Bristol, lying in a pool of blood, absolutely motionless. From where I was sitting, his body looked intact, but I knew all that blood had to be coming from somewhere. What had Cryder done to him, exactly?

I didn't really want to know.

"Cryder," I said suddenly, as it hit me. "The bodies we've seen around town. The body you and I found in the park... Was that Bristol?"

He hesitated. "I don't know that for sure. I think it probably was, yes."

"But you don't know for sure?'

"I'm...fairly sure."

"You mean it might have been someone else? There could be... more of them?'

He rested a hand on my cheek. "There are more of us, Rena."

Us. I shivered. The panic was rising in my stomach again. I wasn't really safe yet, was I? Bristol was dead, yes, but presumably whatever was in my blood that made him want me so badly was still there. Was it only a matter of time, then, until another attacker came to kill me?

Would I ever truly be safe again?

Cryder seemed to hear my thoughts. "It's all right," he said. "I'll take care of it, Rena."

"Cecile could have died because of me."

"She's going to be all right."

I turned to see Cecile sitting upright. Drake was supporting her with a hand on her back and watching her solicitously. She had tears in her eyes, and she was shivering like a person recovering from the flu, but otherwise she seemed fine. "Cecile!" I gasped in relief.

"Rena!"

She was out of Drake's arms, across the clearing, and wrapping her arms around me in a flash. I clung to her, almost afraid to let go. "Cecile, my God. I was so scared. I was so worried."

"You're babbling," she said, laughing a little.

"I'm babbling?"

"I'm fine." She held out her arms, turning them one way and then they other as if to show me that they were intact.

I batted them aside and inspected her hairline. "You're not bleeding anymore."

"Was I?"

"Does your head hurt?" I asked.

She thought about it, lifting a hand gently to her temple. "No," she said finally. "It really doesn't."

"But..." But Bristol had thrown her to the ground. But I was sure her head had struck a rock. "I thought you were dead," I said again, rather dumbly.

"Oh, honey." Cecile embraced me. "Of course, I wasn't dead."

"You were unconscious."

"That's not dead."

"But he said..."

"Who said?"

"Drake." I pointed at him, squatted away from us across the clearing, watching us like we were a curiosity.

"Is that his name? Like a duck? What a weird name."

"Cecile!"

"Sorry, sorry." She snapped her focus back to me. "What did the duck say?"

"He said you would die, if..."

"If what?"

I found myself at a loss for words. Cecile didn't know

what Drake had done. Could I really be the one to tell her what I had decided on her behalf? What if she was angry? She would have every right to be—I had let a total stranger bleed into her mouth because he said she was dying and that would help. Free of context, it sounded insane. What if he'd given her hepatitis or something? What if he was just some crazy drifter who wanted to see if he could convince a desperate, stupid girl to poison her best friend?

But that didn't explain the fangs.

I started to breathe easier. For the first time, the fangs that had been so alien and terrifying on Bristol brought me comfort. Whatever Drake was, whatever he had done, it was okay that I didn't understand it. There was so much that I didn't understand. Working from incomplete information, I had done the best I could for Cecile. She would understand that. After all, she had done the same when Cryder had given her the mysterious drink for me.

What was in that drink? I got chills, suddenly.

To Cecile I said, "Drake said you would die unless I let him give you blood."

She frowned. "Like a transfusion?"

"Like...orally."

She made a face. "That's disgusting."

"I know. I thought you were dying, Cecile."

"She was dying," Drake spoke up. "Cecile, there's no blood on you now, there's no wound, but look here. Look on the ground."

We both looked. Sure enough, the earth where Cecile

had lain was stained dark. Drake's white shirt also bore bloodstains, and there they appeared deep red. It was nightmarish.

Cecile was staring. "That's all...mine?" She looked to me for confirmation, and I could see she was having trouble believing it. "But I'm not even hurt..."

"You were," I said. "Cecile, whatever else this is, that part is definitely true. You were knocked out, you were bleeding, and I honestly believed him when he told me you were going to die." I drew a breath. "I still believe it, I think."

Cecile nodded. "Then you did what you had to do."

"Yeah?" All the tension seemed to rush out of my body. I hadn't realized how anxious I truly was about Cecile's reaction to what I'd allowed.

She laughed a little and hugged me. "Of course, Rena. I would have done the same if it had been you. I'd never let you die; you know that. Not if there was any other way."

"I love you," I whispered into her hair.

"You too, goofball."

Remembering the other part of what Drake had said, I held her back at arm's length and studied her. He had told me that saving Cecile's life would come at the cost of making her "like him." I thought of his fangs, and of Bristol's incredible strength and speed, and I examined my best friend. She was still Cecile, still the girl I'd known all my life. And yet, something felt different, slightly off. I remembered with a start how quickly she'd crossed the clearing from Drake to me. Had it truly been as fast as I was imagining? Was I overdramatizing the moment in my mind? Or had she really been as fast as Bristol?

"What?" asked Cecile, raising an eyebrow at me. I'd been staring at her too long.

"Nothing." I smiled. "I'm just glad you're okay. We should head home."

As Cryder and Drake led the way out of the clearing, though, I kept thinking about Cecile, watching her closely when her eyes were focused elsewhere.

Did she have fangs now? I couldn't ask her to show me. It would be too macabre, for her to find out that way. Telling her what I'd allowed Drake to do while she was unconscious was one thing. Telling her she'd been irrevocably altered by it...that was something else altogether. I didn't know enough to break that news. Drake, or perhaps Cryder, would have to explain.

And I hoped they would do it soon. Somebody really needed to start explaining what was going on around here, why my life had been so transformed over the past few weeks that I barely recognized it—or myself—anymore. Why had these strangers come to our town in the first place, and why had Bristol killed so many and left their bodies around? What was the strange concoction that Cryder had been so adamant that I drink, and why had it had such a positive effect—for it had, there was no denying that—on my health?

And what were they? What was Cryder really? The changing eye color, the speed and power, the blood obsession, and, of course, the fangs...it all added up to one thing, one creature I'd always known was the stuff of myth and fantasy. And yet here they were, standing in the clearing with me and Cecile, watching us.

Vampires.

What in the world could they possibly want with me?

Chapter Thirteen

I NEEDED ANSWERS TO SO MANY QUESTIONS. But before I could ask, a gust of wind seemed to sweep the clearing. Dust filled my mouth. I coughed, trying to clear it, and felt a hand—Cecile's—begin to rub circles on my back.

When I managed to drive my eyelids up, everything had changed.

The dirt by my feet, which had been soaked with Cecile's blood only a moment before, was now unsullied. It was as if nothing had ever happened here.

"Oh no," Drake murmured.

"What is it?' Cryder asked. We all turned.

Drake was staring at the spot where Bristol's body had lain. The ground there, too, was pristine. Just bits of grass speckling the forest floor.

Bristol's body had vanished.

For the first time, Cryder appeared truly shaken. "What do you suppose that means?'

"I don't know," Drake said.

"He is dead, isn't he?" The fear rearing up inside me again sent a tremor through my voice.

"There's no reason to think otherwise," Drake said. He sounded very reassuring, but I'd heard the anxiety in his tone before. Even if Bristol was dead, that didn't necessarily mean we had nothing left to worry about.

But it was hard to worry too much right now. I'd been afraid of losing my life today, and with Bristol gone, I felt for the first time in hours that I was truly among friends. True, I didn't know Drake or even Cryder all that well, but it was hard to imagine them wishing me harm. Whatever had happened, I thought, maybe it was best to simply not look too closely. Maybe the lesson here was to be grateful for the fact that I was alive and not try to dig into the mysteries of the universe. After all, wasn't that what had gotten me into trouble in the first place?

I turned my mind to another mystery instead—how were we going to get home?

"How did you get here?" Cryder asked, when I voiced the question. He seemed surprised that this was even an issue. But then, I thought, noting a slight bitterness in my own mind, it was probably easy not to worry about transportation when you could run as fast as he could. Why did Cryder even own a car? It was probably some macho guy thing.

"We drove," Cecile supplied. "But the car broke down."

"Can you take me to it?" Drake said. "I know a thing or two about cars."

"I know a thing or two about cars, too," Cecile said, her

eyes narrowing a little. "What do you think, I need a man to change my tires for me?"

"Were you able to fix whatever's wrong with it?" Drake asked.

Cecile was silent for a moment. "No," she admitted.

"Would you mind if I just take a look?"

She sighed. "Oh, all right," she conceded.

We all followed her back in the direction we had come. As we walked, I couldn't help but notice the change that had come over my best friend. Her usually frizzy hair was shiny and bouncy. Her skin was positively radiant, seeming to give off a glow even in the late afternoon light. She was even well put together and clean, which was frankly shocking after all we'd been through. I knew I didn't look tidy at all. I tried to run a hand through my hair and came away holding a stick. My hands and arms were covered with dirt. I was a mess. Cecile was immaculate.

How could that be?

We seemed to reach the car very quickly. I was surprised, given how long our flight through the woods had seemed. Were we all moving faster than usual? I sure wasn't capable of the high speeds I'd seen from Cryder, but Drake probably was, and as for Cecile, she was skipping along like she didn't know what her feet were doing. Maybe it was just the fact that I was relaxed now and not being chased by a psychopath. That would probably make anyone feel less aware of time passing.

The car was right where we'd left it. "Do you have a

spare tire?" Drake asked.

"I don't know," Cecile said stiffly. She really didn't know anything about cars. A laugh welled up in my throat, but I pushed it down—she wouldn't appreciate my finding humor in that. It was just so very Cecile to insist that she was perfectly capable of handling everything, even when she wasn't.

Drake checked the trunk of the car and found the spare and a jack. He quickly had the car propped up and began screwing the lug nuts off the tire with his bare hand.

"Um," I said, staring. "Don't you need a tool to do that?"

"I didn't see a lug wrench back there," he said. "It's all right, I can handle it."

I turned to Cryder. "At some point we're going to have to talk about all this, you know."

"All what?"

"Don't give me that."

"What am I giving you?"

"You know perfectly well all what. The fact that he can unscrew those with his bare hands. The way you guys run. How strong you are. The...the fangs." I swallowed. "Everything."

"Oh." Cryder nodded slowly. "Right. Of course. Okay."

"I mean soon, Cryder."

"Soon, yes."

"Soon like today."

"We'll go back to our house," Drake said, from where he was crouched on the ground. I hadn't realized he was listening. "It's the best place to talk in private."

"You two live together?' Cecile asked, raising an eyebrow at each of them in turn. "Are you like…together?'

"Of course not," Cryder said, looking scandalized.

"There wouldn't be anything wrong with that," Cecile said.

"There would be something wrong with my courting Rena if I was already involved with someone else," he pointed out.

Cecile mimed a spit take. "Courting? What are you going to do, ask her to the debutante ball?'

"If there was a debutante ball," Cryder said, now looking thoroughly annoyed, "I would ask her." He turned to Drake. "And I'm not sure bringing them to our house is the best idea right now, Drake."

"Why not?' he asked, tightening the final lug nut on the new tire. He got to his feet and dusted off his hands on the knees of his pants. "It's the safest place."

"Everything's bound to come out if we go there," Cryder hedged.

"That's for the best," Drake said. "Cecile needs to know everything now."

"But, Rena."

"It's about time you told me what's going on, Cryder," I interjected. "I don't appreciate being kept in the dark like this, especially about things that are so obviously important." I shook slightly, but I pushed it aside. So much had happened in such a short period of time.

Drake's eyes were soft. "You can't really shield her any longer, Cryder. Not after what's just happened. She deserves to know."

"Thank you," I said, but a thrill of fear shot through me. What was I about to discover? What had Cryder thought I needed protecting from?

I was about to ask, but suddenly the world swam, and the ground seemed to rush up at me. I felt like I was falling in slow motion, and as my vision blacked out, I had time to realize it had been almost a full day since I'd had any of Cryder's mystery concoction. Hands grabbed my shoulders and I thought I heard someone calling my name from far away, but I couldn't answer. I couldn't even think of what to say.

Then they were gone.

And I heard a different voice.

Dad.

He was singing along with the radio, replacing Bobby Darin's classic lyrics with some riff about the town we were passing through, and I was laughing...but it wasn't me. It was young-me, me as I had been before anything had happened, me before I knew how dark life could get. Watching the scene, I wanted to wrap my arms around that little girl and protect her from everything I knew lay in her future, but I was utterly helpless. I could do nothing but watch. I watched as the car swerved and the lights flashed, and through my pounding ears came the horrible crunch of metal that sometimes filled my deepest nightmares. But I wasn't asleep this time. I couldn't claw my way out of whatever this was. I couldn't depend on

Cecile to burst in and wake me up.

The scene shifted. I was outside the car, sitting on the grass beside my younger self, who was crying. There were sirens, and screams, and Mom—

Mom?

No. She'd died in the car. She wasn't in this part of the memory.

But I heard her. She was upset—of course she was upset, we'd been in a crash, Dad was—but she was angry. She was yelling at someone. Why was she so angry? Was it the other driver? I didn't understand. I felt like I was a little kid all over again, staring at the chaos of this scene, utterly unable to take in what had happened and was continuing to happen. None of it made any sense.

Against my better judgement, I tried to look toward the car. More than anything, I wanted to avoid seeing the mangled wreckage that had stolen my former life. But I had to know what was happening.

As soon as I turned my eyes toward the vehicle, though, I was met by a blinding light. I had to close my eyes immediately. It was too painful to look. Was that psychosomatic? I tried to peek again and got the same result. My mind wasn't playing tricks on me, then—it was a genuine light preventing me from seeing anything that was going on. My mother was over there—I could still hear her yelling—but I couldn't go to her or even look at her. Had that happened? Was this how it had really been, the day of the accident? It couldn't have been. I would have remembered something so strange and unsettling.

Wouldn't I?

Could this have happened, but I'd blocked it out or simply forgotten in the wake of all the other trauma of that day? Was that possible?

A hand took hold of my arm—it was gentle, not rough—and pulled me close. I was lifted into strong, capable arms. That felt familiar. This happened. I was sure of it, even though I didn't know exactly how I knew.

"Rena!" my mother screamed. I wanted to go to her. I struggled against the arms that were holding me, but it felt as if I'd become my young self. Whoever had me was so strong that my own strength was childlike...or maybe my perception was simply merging with the memory. Whatever it was, I couldn't get away. Instead, I was pulled closer, held against someone who smelled clean and earthy, with a hint of smoke. Like the woods.

Like Cryder.

Another shift.

Now I was in a hospital room. I remembered this part. The machines were beeping. I was wearing a hospital gown that didn't cover me adequately and lying on a pillow that was so flat it might as well have not been there at all. My arm throbbed from the IV. I could feel it nestled under my skin, itching and pulling at me uncomfortably. But all of that was eclipsed by the horrible knowledge of the crash that came rushing back to me, and the understanding that I was alone in the world. My parents were gone.

But Mom was outside the car.

I felt short of breath.

Had she survived the crash? Could she be alive after all?

How could that be? Surely, she would have come to find me. Cecile's house had to be the first place anyone would look. I hadn't been hidden. No. I couldn't believe this. If Mom was alive, she wouldn't have let me believe otherwise even for a day. She would have come for me. Whatever I was experiencing, it was a dream, not a memory. It hadn't happened this way, and I couldn't allow myself to be suckered into thinking like this.

I couldn't....

I heard soft voices. "She's coming around," someone said.

I blinked my eyes open.

The hospital was gone. I was on the ground beside the car, staring up at three concerned faces. "Rena!" Cecile gasped. "Are you all right?"

I wanted to answer her, but my vision swam. I closed my eyes.

"We need to get her inside," Drake said, sounding alarmed. "Put her in the car, Cryder."

"Just a minute," Cryder said. He was holding me up, one arm under my shoulders and the other brushing the hair out of my face. "We can take a minute here. She's dizzy."

I was dizzy. I was glad he'd said so.

"Take a deep breath, Rena," Cryder advised. His voice was gentle. "Get some air."

I closed my eyes and did as he'd advised...and immediately was hit with that woodsy scent from the memory, or vision, or whatever I'd seen. Cryder! I snapped my eyes open, which made the world spin again, but I had to know. "You! You were there?"

"What?" There was fear in Cecile's voice. "What is she talking about?"

"Oh, Rena..." Cryder breathed.

"You were at the crash, weren't you? I... you saved me?" Had he been the one to take me away from the car, to the hospital? Was it possible?

The implications were overwhelming. I wanted to hear Cryder's answer, but it was all too much—the dizziness, the colors disappearing around me, the weakness drowning me. I let my eyes slip closed and succumbed once again.

This time, there was only darkness.

Chapter Fourteen

` THE FIRST THING TO PENETRATE THE blackness was the smell of coffee. Cecile's coffee. I'd have known it anywhere. She always added nutmeg to the brew, called it her secret recipe. Everyone who had ever tried it loved it.

Everyone loved Cecile.

A moment later I heard her voice. I couldn't make out what she was saying, but I knew I'd recognize that strident tone and whisper that couldn't quite contain itself anywhere. It brought to mind every time she'd hissed a secret across the aisle to me during school, insistent that whatever she had to say couldn't wait.

I opened my eyes.

I was in a bedroom I didn't recognize, with pale yellow walls and mahogany furnishings, lit by a dim light. The room was empty. But I could hear Cecile's voice not far away. A moment later, Cryder spoke. They must have been just outside the door.

I pushed back the comforter and got to my feet, slowly,

because I expected the dizziness to wash over me as soon as I stood up. But to my surprise, I felt fine. It was as if I'd gotten a hearty meal and a full night's sleep. How long was I out? Was it possible I'd slept through the night?

A cracked door in the corner of the room proved to lead to a bathroom. I stepped to the sink, turned it on, and splashed some cold water on my face.

Whoa.

The water felt…

Well, it felt rich. I wasn't sure how else to describe it. It was like sinking into a soft down mattress, biting into a spoon full of whipped cream, and stroking your skin with silk, all rolled into one. I jerked back, startled, and wiped my face on my arm. Then, cautiously, I held my hand under the water. It produced the same feeling.

What is this? Wherever we were—Drake and Cryder's house? Had we gone there?—something was very strange about the water. I steeled myself and washed my face, scrubbing extra hard with my hands to distract from the strange, frightening feel of the water.

Then I looked up at the mirror.

What?

It was me that much was clear. Same eyes, same birthmark above my mouth. The reflection in the mirror moved when I did. And yet something was different. It was something subtle, yet somehow significant enough that I almost thought I was looking at a different person. When was the last time I'd gotten out of bed with my hair in such perfect condition? When was the last time my skin had been so clear and even? It was like my idealized version of myself. And come to think of it…hadn't I had bruises around my neck? I pulled at the collar of my shirt, checking, gently touching my skin. Nothing. I was bruise-free.

What the hell?

I closed my eyes, trying to make sense of it all, but behind my eyelids the only thing I could see was the crashed car that had risen in my memory the night before. And there was my mom, screaming, yelling—

Fighting.

She was fighting.

And as she turned to me, the sun flashed and revealed her golden eyes, her bared fangs.

Mom?

Cryder, young but still powerful. He'd been there, too. I saw him clearly now, darting past the car, lifting me in his arms. I remembered being placed in a car. Then nothing.

And then the hospital.

He drove me to the hospital. I'd always assumed it had been an ambulance. I'd never asked. But it had been Cryder all along.

How could that be?

I made my way out of the bathroom, switching off the light. I was half tempted to get back into bed and see if the world made more sense when I woke up again. But I couldn't. It was time for answers.

I stepped out into the hall.

Cecile, Cryder, and Drake were there, waiting for me. Everyone looked up from where they sat in the hallway.

I could tell they'd been up all night, but not in any of the usual ways. Nobody was red-eyed or tired looking. Nobody had messed up hair or wrinkled clothing. Instead, it was in the way they reacted to me, as if they were all exhaling collectively, letting out a breath that had been held for far too long. They'd been worrying about me, I realized. These people—all of them—truly cared what happened to me.

"Okay," I said. "Let's talk."

***

I wanted coffee, but Drake said no.

"She needs to be taking in as much of the mixture as possible right now," he said, speaking to Cryder over his shoulder. "If she's hungry or thirsty, prepare her some."

"I am right here, you know," I said, glaring at them.

Drake nodded. "I apologize. You should know as well. The drink Cryder is preparing for you is what's kept you alive and well during recent days."

"Okay," I said. "I get that. I mean, I do always feel better after I drink it. But what is it? Vitamins?'

"Not exactly."

Cryder joined us at the table and placed a cup before me. "I don't know if she's ready to hear this, Drake."

"She has to," he said evenly. "It's time."

Cryder nodded slowly. "Rena, that cup contains a blood mixture. It's half human blood and half my blood."

I stared.

"It's important that you drink it," he said anxiously.

"Human blood?" I could barely form the words on my lips.

"Rena…"

"How did you get that? Did you kill someone?"

"No. No, of course not. And I promise I'll explain everything if you give me time, but right now, please, just drink. You'll get sick again if you don't."

"Drink blood."

Cecile, who was standing with her back to the wall, spoke up. "It's what you've been drinking this whole time," she said, softly.

I lifted the cup slowly to my lips, tipped it, and let the liquid touch my tongue. I was prepared to gag…

But it was delicious.

Suddenly I was ravenous. I swallowed the drink in great gulps, consumed by how wonderful it tasted and felt going down. It was only once the cup was empty that my thoughts returned to the fact that I was drinking blood. I shivered a little. Cryder's hand covered mine gently. "Good job," he said. "I knew you could do it."

"You didn't know she could do it," Drake said. "You thought she wasn't ready. I knew she could do it."

"Guys," Cecile snapped. "Tell her the rest now."

"The rest?" I looked from one of them to the next.

Cryder sighed. "Rena, you're one of us now."

"One of you?"

"A vampire."

I pulled my hand back. I knew it. "You're vampires."

"I don't think you're surprised to hear that."

"The fangs. The speed and strength."

"Yes," Drake said. "All of that. But some of what you might have seen and read isn't real."

"What, you don't turn shiny in sunlight?'

"We don't do anything in sunlight. Sunlight doesn't affect us. We can go into churches, and into private homes without being invited. You don't need to stake us in the heart to kill us. We don't sleep in coffins. We aren't monsters."

"Bristol?'

"He's a murderer. There are human murderers, too."

"But you drink blood."

"There are ways to acquire blood without killing," Cryder said. "Donors, for example."

"But—but you eat food," I stammered. I was remembering our date. "I've seen you eat food."

"Sure," Cryder said. "I like food. But I require blood to survive." He met my eyes. "And so, do you, Rena."

"No," I said automatically. "I'm not a vampire."

"You are," Cecile said. "We all are."

"You are?'

"You're the one who let it happen. You gave Drake permission to turn me. He told me all about it," she said, registering the look of surprise on my face. "You gave him permission because you knew I would have died otherwise."

"Cecile…"

"It's all right. I told you before, it was the right choice. I would have done the same thing. But I do wish he had been clearer with us about exactly what would happen." Cecile glared at Drake, but there was no heat behind it. She wasn't really angry. If I knew her, she was just planning to hold this against Drake long enough to make him feel that he owed her one.

"But wait," I said, as the realization hit me. "I wasn't bitten, was I? How did I become a vampire?"

Cryder's hand found mine again. "You've always been one."

"What? No. I can't have. I'm a human."

"You were born to a human father and vampire mother," Drake explained. "As you've come of age, your vampire side has developed and is now fully manifested. That's why we came looking for you."

"To get me to join your...coven? Den? Whatever?"

Cryder and Drake looked at each other and laughed. "We aren't bats," Drake said. "Cryder is the heir in a royal bloodline. I am his cousin and bodyguard."

"You're royals?" This was too much. Not only was Cryder a vampire, he was a prince?

"And so are you," Cryder said.

"What?"

"Your family, too, is extremely powerful. And from the day you were born, Rena, you and I have been intended for each other."

I blinked at him. "We're betrothed?"

"Something like that," Drake said. "Your families have

been great allies for millennia. You two were destined to unite your houses and rule together. As such, your blood is extremely powerful."

"Our blood is powerful? Is all vampire blood powerful?'

"Not in the same way. For example, I am not destined for anyone, even though I share Cryder's royal lineage. My blood doesn't contain the power his does. That's why I was able to use it to change Cecile. Cryder's blood is too precious and dangerous for such a task."

"Charmed, I'm sure," Cecile said sardonically.

"That's also why Cryder's blood is able to revitalize you, Rena. And that's why Bristol was here."

"He wanted my blood," I remember.

"Your blood contains tremendous power. He would have been able to access it."

Cecile shuddered. "I'm glad he's dead."

"Others will come," Drake warned. "Now that Rena is fully vampire, many will hunt for her."

"So, it's just going to be like this from now on? Forever?' I ask. "Vampires showing up wherever I go, trying to kill me? What am I supposed to do? We barely escaped this time! God forbid the next one brings a friend."

Drake nodded. "I wanted you to understand all this because there is a solution to the problem, and I believe it is vital that you accept it."

"What's the solution?' I couldn't believe there could be anything I wouldn't do to extricate myself from these circumstances.

Drake looked to Cryder.

Cryder scooted his chair close to me. "The only way for us to stay safe is to join together," he said, taking my hands in his. "We must fulfill our collective destiny, assume the thrones, and rule together as King and Queen."

Chapter Fifteen

ALL I COULD DO FOR SEVERAL MINUTES was stare. "You're saying my choices are risk death at the hands of violent beasts like Bristol or else marry you and become...Queen of the Underworld?' I finally managed to stammer.

"It's hardly the underworld," Drake said softly. His air was that of a doctor telling a patient that she's not going to die of the terrible thing that's wrong with her, and I could see why he would be a good person to have around. "We live aboveground. The life vampires live day-to-day is surprisingly similar to the life you already know, Rena."

"What about the life of queens?'

"Well," Drake chuckled a little, "that would probably be a bit of an adjustment."

"It could be pretty great, right?' Cecile said. I could tell she was trying to look on the bright side. "We always used to pretend we were princesses, Rena, remember?'

"That was you. I was always the knight."

"Because I made you be the knight. Now you could be the princess."

I closed my eyes. Did I want to be a princess? It seemed so...unreal. But then, what about everything else I'd just been told?

My mother was a vampire.

I was becoming a vampire.

Cryder had been watching me my whole life. Keeping me safe. Ever since the car accident that had changed my life forever, he'd been ensuring that I would be protected, that I would be ready when the time came. And now he was ready to marry me, to share his life and his world with me. All I had to do was say yes.

I wanted to.

But how could I know what I wanted so fast? It didn't make sense; I knew that much. I'd barely known Cryder for weeks, and we'd only had a few significant conversations. Today was probably the first time he'd been truly honest with me. How could I be ready to say yes to his proposal?

I didn't know. I only knew that I felt something deep within me, something I was powerless to resist. Maybe it was the blood connection we already shared, coursing through my veins and filling my heart. Maybe it was the knowledge that he had always been a presence in my life, even if I hadn't realized it. Maybe it was just those gorgeous blue eyes, watching me from across the room. They pulled me in, magnetically, and before I could even consider what I was doing I was crossing the room, closing the distance between us, reaching up for him and bringing his lips to mine.

It was the most amazing kiss of my life. It was the first kiss I'd ever initiated myself. Cryder seemed momentarily surprised, then kissed me back with a gentle force that seemed as if it belonged to nature, like the current of a river. I reached up and cupped his face with both hands, standing on my toes to give us a better angle. His arms twined around my waist. He could lift me off the ground, I knew, but he didn't, and I was glad. In this moment, possibly for the first time since I'd known him, we were on a level playing field, each of us giving and taking in equal measure.

Yes. I could be with him.

As we separated, our eyes met and I laughed a little, awkwardly. Cryder wiped a tear from my cheek with his thumb. I hadn't realized I was crying.

"Was that okay?" Cryder asked, concern in his eyes.

I nodded, at a loss for words. We'd kissed before, of course, but something was different now. I couldn't put my finger on it. "I'm just emotional…with the whole idea of agreeing to marry you. Everything feels stronger, deeper, now that I'm…what I am now."

Vampire, my mind whispered.

Could it be? I knew I must be more vampire—less human—than I had been at the time of our last kiss. After all, look what had happened to Cecile. A few drops of Drake's blood and she was as much a vampire as any of them. My case was different than hers, of course. My transition had been more gradual. I assumed that was because of my human father.

But now I had been drinking Cryder's blood for weeks.

I've been drinking Cryder's blood. To my astonishment, the idea didn't make me shudder. It actually made me feel more bonded to him. I must be a vampire.

Regardless, I decided, whatever was making me feel this way toward Cryder could only be a good thing, particularly if it brought this extra element to the kisses we shared. I felt the love and the bond between us like a current, impossible to resist, and I gave in and let myself drift back into his arms. "I'm good," I whispered. "Everything's so good."

He smiled. "I think so too."

I rested my head against his chest, unable to get over how natural this felt. It was like coming home. It was more than that. It was like discovering a home I'd always longed for, but never known I had.

I could have stayed here forever. I felt utterly safe in his arms, indifferent to the world around me, to the dangers Cryder and Drake had just outlined. I even found myself forgetting the other people in the room. But all too soon, Cryder released me and stepped back. "There will be time," he said softly, and I understood what he meant. Now that we had found each other—or, more accurately, now that I had found him—we could spend as much time as necessary getting to know each other. Learning each other. We didn't have to cling together in this room in front of our friends. Starting today, we would be together no matter where we were.

"What do we do now?' I asked him.

"What do you mean?'

"I'm assuming we don't...you know. Go on a date." I felt myself blushing. I didn't even know how to ask a guy out under normal circumstances, and these were anything but normal. I had to admit, though, that the idea of a date was incredibly appealing. How wonderful would it be to attend prom with Cryder on my arm? How great would it be to go out to a movie and share a tub of popcorn, cuddling together and whispering about the actors and plot? Or a walk through the woods? Of course, with other vampires chasing us for the value of our blood, we could hardly go walking in the woods. "I'm guessing we have to do something more official than that, right? Go back to your home country? Or, do you even have a home country? Are you American?' I realized how little I knew about him. He certainly sounded American. Was all the foreignness I picked up from these two simply a function of their inhumanity? America didn't have kings and queens, though. That much, I was sure of.

Drake stepped forward. "You're right in thinking we have to leave the country, Rena. But it has nothing to do with making things official. As far as the customs of our people are concerned, your acceptance of Cryder's proposal is all that's needed. But now that the word is out that the two of you are here, it's no longer safe to put down roots on this continent."

"Where will we go?' I asked. My mind was racing. Leaving the country would mean leaving behind everything I knew. But did I really have that many attachments here? The few friends I'd made throughout school, I knew, would be easy to leave behind. Cecile was the only one I couldn't stand to say goodbye to, and as a new vampire, she would likely be coming with me. When I thought about it that way, suddenly the future seemed full of hope and possibility. It was exciting. Traveling to a foreign land, learning new customs and meeting new people...it was the kind of thing many high school students dreamed about, but few were lucky enough to experience. And I would be royalty, welcomed by the new people I would meet. I would be their queen.

"You can finish out the school year," Cryder said. "The security measures we have in place ought to be enough to protect you. And it will take time for word of Bristol's death to spread, and for his clan to send more out after him. You have only a few weeks left, right?'

"Yes," I said. "I could probably leave now."

"There's no need. Graduate. Get your diploma. You'll be glad you did."

I raised an eyebrow at him. "Do I need a degree to be a vampire queen?'

"You never know when your education will come in handy," Drake said with a serious look.

"Okay, so fine. I'll finish school. What happens after that?'

"After that," Cryder said, "the four of us will return to my ancestral home."

"Me too?' Cecile asked.

"Yes," Cryder confirmed, and my heart soared a little. I wouldn't be alone in the days to come. "It's not safe for you here either anymore, now that you're a known associate of

Rena. And you belong among other vampires. We can guide you as you learn to live your new life."

"My family is here," Cecile said, biting her lip.

"You'll have a new family with us."

"What happens when we get there?" I asked.

"You will undergo the dhampir rituals of our clan."

"Dhampir?"

"Part human, part vampire," Drake clarified.

"There's a name for that? Is it common?" I asked.

"No," Cryder said. "In fact, it's very uncommon. The last one in recorded history was over a hundred years ago. And because of your nature, the rituals you must undergo will be very trying—very painful—for you. But they are necessary. By the time it's over, you'll have been fully transformed into the vampire queen you were meant to be. Your strength and power will increase exponentially, and you will be fully prepared to rule over the people of our bloodline."

I bit my lip. Very painful. It sounded terrifying. But the promise of attaining my full strength—a strength, I now realized, I was born to possess—fueled my resolve to go through with it. And then there was the allure of ruling at Cryder's side, of being together with him in the days to come. When I thought about it that way, I knew I could survive whatever trials lay ahead. I could do whatever it took to fulfill my destiny and take my place as Cryder's queen.

"We'll journey to Italy," Cryder said. "There, we will find the rest of my family and our blood clan."

"Right. No problem." I took a deep breath. "So, I just

have to survive the rest of high school, graduate, go to Italy, and learn to be queen of the vampires. I can do that."

"I'll be with you all the way," Cecile said, taking my hand.

"We all will," Drake said. "The protection you'll require against rogue vampires is best handled by groups. As long as we all stick together, we'll be safe."

"What about your mom?' I asked Cecile.

She gave me a tight smile. "I'll just tell her we're traveling with friends. She knew it was a possibility. I'd talked about it before. And then we'll figure out the rest as we go along."

I looked from one of them to the next. My friends. My new family. And Cryder, my fiancé. The king to my queen. I couldn't believe this was my life. And yet, there was a part of me—a part of me that felt stronger and more powerful with each passing moment—that couldn't wait to get started.

I smiled and felt the tug of my blood. "Let's do this."

ABOUT THE AUTHOR

Tiffany Heiser is the author of Yearn for Blood, the first book in the Blood Origins series. She was born in Killeen, TX. She spent her early years writing and reading, living in fantasy worlds and writing out her feelings in poems.

She grew up with her parents doting on her creative abilities and pushing her to continue doing what she always loved to do. Raised in a small town in Central Texas where she resides ow with her son, their dog, and her son's hamster-along with the plethora of notepads, pens, and books as she continues her dream of writing.

Yearn for Blood

Willow Moon Publishing